I0545731

TAINTED

THE SHATTERED G-CODE

U. E. Wynn

Copyright © 2019 U. E. Wynn
All rights reserved. No part of this material may be reproduced or altered in any
form or by any means, electronic, mechanical, photocopying, recording or
otherwise without prior written permission of the writer.

This book is a work of fiction. All of the characters, organizations, and events
portrayed in this novel are either products of the author's imagination or are used
fictitiously.

All rights reserved. No part of this publication may be reproduced, stored in a
retrieval system, or transmitted in any form or by any means, electronic,
mechanical, photocopying, recording, or otherwise, without the prior written
permission of the publisher.

Cover designed by Dynasty's Visionary Designs
www.facebook.com/dynastys.coverme

ISBN-13: 978-1-7320325-5-2
ISBN-10: 1-7320325-5-2

DEDICATION

First and foremost, I must thank the most high for waking me and giving me the vision to express what I have endured. This book is a tribute to two men who never crossed paths, but both equally made a positive impact in my life.

Long live Brooklyn's finest "PRIME"! I know you're gonna keep those demons off me, and it's always and forever "PRIMETIME."

REST EASY to the heart and soul of Greensboro N.C "TEFLON." I poured a bottle of Henny and drank a bottle with the bros. It was like old times. #FUCKCANCER!

This last gesture of gratitude is for a friend who has become more like a sister. Yooo, Emily, thanks for just being you. I know you don't know this, but most days you're words are the only positive gestures I receive and I will always be grateful!

Rest easy Nipsey Hussle. A king gone before his time.

U.E. Wynn,

ABOUT THE AUTHOR

U.E. Wynn

A self-educated, business savvy, humble entrepreneur was counted out at a young age by his peers, teachers, and family members. After enduring life altering events that would destroy and/or diminish any individual, he chose to overcome and excel. He turned what would be deemed a negative into a positive. He reevaluated himself and reclaimed a positive position within society.

U.E. Wynn is the founder of 501C nonprofit, Save a H.O.M.I.E. Inc. and an active activist within the community. He continues to assist disenfranchised youth, feed and clothe the homeless and bring forth literacy to the illiterate. Wynn also helps in providing a positive, productive and social atmosphere for the youth to unwind and enjoy themselves throughout the Carolinas via events, concerts and parties.

This is Wynn's second novel presenting you with a page turning, nail biting, exotic read.

TAINTED

Prologue

"Baby, tonight was the greatest. I can't wait until we get inside so I can give you my present," Vanessa said as they stopped at a red light. She reached over and took Too-reel's right hand, placing it between her warm, soft legs. Too-reel extended his arm further until his fingertip was greeted by her warm moistness.

"As cold as it is outside, you're not wearing any panties! You're a little freak!" he teased as he pulled off from the green light. He slipped his middle finger into her velvety moistness. Skillfully, he maneuvered his finger around, touching off a ripple effect of sensations. Then he abruptly removed it, placing it into his mouth, eyes ablaze with the promise of erotic mischief.

"I'm your little freak," she retorted, staring at him longingly as she stuck two fingers inside herself and wiggled them around as he had. She removed her fingers that were glazed with her secretions, sticking them into her mouth, and sucked on them as if they were dipped in honey. "Tonight can be our pre-honeymoon."

Too-reel smiled and licked his lips as he savored the thoughts of things he and Vanessa were about to do. He anxiously, but expertly, pulled the 2010 Cadillac Escalade inside his garage. The garage door automatically closed as if sensing the urgency of the upcoming moment.

A few hours ago, Too-reel had proposed to Vanessa, and she had accepted. They had met over three years ago and had been an item for the last two and a half years. He had fallen deeply in love with the five-feet-six-inch, honey-brown complexioned beauty with forest green cat eyes. Vanessa was petite with the body of a gymnast. Not one to fall for a pretty face and a phat ass, Too-reel had been conquered by her personality. And, for once in his life, he had let down his guard and taken a chance on love. Once his mother met

Vanessa and gave her approval, everything was a go. He was finally ready to get married.

Too-reel exited his truck and walked over to the passenger side to open Vanessa's door. When she unbuckled her seatbelt, she fell straight out of the truck, laughing, still tipsy from all the champagne they had drunk.

"Careful now, I'm going to need you conscious for what we're about to do." He gently steadied her on her feet, placing his arms around her back to brace her against his body as they walked toward the door that led inside his house.

"FBI, put your hands in the air!" were the words that greeted them as Too-reel unlocked the door to his house. Ten federal agents stood in his living room and kitchen area, all with guns pointed at him and Vanessa.

"I hope you have a warrant," Too-reel calmly replied, unfazed by the sight confronting him. He had always known they would eventually come for him, one day. Guess that day was today.

"You don't worry about that," the lead agent responded. "Agent Tyson, would you do us the honors?"

Vanessa grabbed Too-reel's hand and twisted it around his back while forcing his body against the wall. She was handed a pair of cuffs, which she slapped on his wrists. Too-reel was devastated, but his face showed no emotions. Vanessa had dreaded this day for the last year. She had really fallen in love with Too-reel, but she also had a job to do.

Two agents grabbed Too-reel and turned him around as they walked him back to his garage. Vanessa held her head down as he passed her. She was unable to meet his gaze.

Too-reel was tossed into the backseat of his own truck. Four agents joined him—two in the front, and one on each side of him as they reversed out of his garage.

Too-reel was taken to a private building that was used as a federal conference office. He was ushered into a drab room and shoved into a metal chair where they left his hands cuffed behind his back.

After a short time, a Caucasian gentleman wearing a beige Armani suit with gold cufflinks, a skinny, blood red tie, and beige snakeskin shoes entered the room. *This guy looks more like a plastic surgeon than an agent*, Too-reel thought. The man's bronzed skin made him out to be the regular tanner he was, while his sky blue eyes, jet-black hair, and chiseled face made him look like a trendier, but older version of Superman.

"Mr. Cobe, my name is Jerol Highmon. I'm not going to waste your time or mine. You know how this works. I can either be your life support or your undertaker. It's all up to you."

"You must really not know who the fuck you're talking to. Death before dishonor, bitch!" Too-reel replied.

"I know exactly who you are, but let's see how you act when that death and dishonor pertain to your mother." Jerol flipped a switch, and the light came on behind a two-way mirror. Too-reel leaped out of his seat, his heart almost bursting from his chest as he saw, to his horror, his mother handcuffed and sitting in the next room with her head bent, palms pressed tightly against her eyes. She was obviously praying.

"What does she have to do with this?" Too-reel yelled.

"She's an accessory to your drug empire. How else would she be able to afford that house she lives in and have that kind of money in her bank account? That's enough to put her away for twenty years unless she can prove how she made it, which, by her employment records, she only makes twenty-four thousand dollars a year as an assistant nurse. I'll hit her for money laundering and prosecute her to the fullest."

"You can't do that!"

"I can and I will. But you don't have to worry. She won't live out her sentence. She's an old woman. We can do this your way or mine. I'll be back in a minute. You can answer me then." Jerol exited the room, leaving Too-reel with his rampaging thoughts.

Too-reel looked at his mother as she sat patiently in the other room. No doubt he knew she was putting her trust in the Lord's hand. At least that was what she would say. He never expected them to come at him from this angle. He was momentarily stuck. He was ready and willing to face any outcome of the game, whether it was death in the streets or life in prison, but he was not prepared for this! How could he let his mother suffer by his hand? She was everything to him.

Jerol Highmon watched from another room with a smirk on his face. Instead of sending guys like Too-reel away for life in prison, he got his satisfaction from breaking them down and turning them into what they despised the most—a snitch. The way he saw it, why waste taxpayers' money to take care of these guys for the rest of their pathetic lives, in the process, glorifying their names in the streets so other young punks idolize them and follow in their footsteps as so-called riders? The system wasn't working. Now it was time to do things his way. Since Too-reel was feared and well respected in the streets, Jerol knew turning him would make snitching seem acceptable to many hustlers.

After watching Too-reel wrestle with his guilty conscience, Jerol slipped back into the room, startling his prey. "Have you made your decision?" he asked.

After a long pause, Too-reel met Jerol's mocking gaze with vengeance in his eyes. "What do you want?"

Jerol smiled.

****

"Good work tonight, Tyson," a fellow agent congratulated.

"Thanks, Graey."

"Hey, Christal, it's karaoke night at the bar and grill. Why don't you join us?" another agent asked Christal Tyson, aka Vanessa Mores.

"No, thanks. Maybe next time. I haven't been home in a year, and it's been a long night."

"It's never easy coming out of deep cover. I understand, kid. Go get some rest." The group of men left, talking loudly as they headed toward the parking garage.

Vanessa walked to her vehicle in the parking garage. It was a candy-red, H3 Hummer Too-reel had bought her for her last birthday. When she got inside and turned on the ignition, a song blared from the speakers, startling her momentarily. She quickly adjusted the volume. Chris Brown's "Say Goodbye" was playing. That was her and Too-reel's song. They used to sing it out loud every time it came on.

She suddenly started crying as she rested her head on the steering wheel. She sobbed like a little girl. This was her first deep-cover operation, and she had fallen hard. As much as she tried to suppress her feelings for Too-reel, she couldn't. Never before had she met a person like him. He was so cold to most people, yet so compassionate with her. The so-called ruthless drug dealer had unlocked a part of her that was previously unexplored. He made her feel things she'd never thought she would feel.

9

And she'd betrayed his trust by stabbing him in his back and heart. She knew that, without her, the Feds would never have gotten close to him. Too-reel was the streets. He honored its codes and also enforced them. He lived by them and would die for them. Arresting him alone wouldn't have done any good. One of his loyal foot soldiers would have just taken his place and forged ahead twice as hard. That was how he had bred them.

Vanessa was now torn between her job and her feelings, although her mission was over. She was thinking about putting in for a transfer and starting over. She used the sleeve of her jacket to wipe away tears as she pulled out of the garage.

Chapter 1

"Yo, Blue, fire up! A nigga ain't blow all morning."

"Hype, you know we're not smoking while we've got all this money in here with us. You know the rules. You trying to make Too-reel kill us?" Blue asked as he glanced over at his man in the passenger seat.

"Shit, he might kill me, but he ain't going to do shit to you. Don't you see how that nigga trusts you? I know we got over three hundred thousand dollars in here with us right now," Hype whistled.

"That's what it's all about, my nigga. Trust. Too-reel told me that in this game, you trust no one, but ironically, at the same time, we work off trust. Yo, here goes this fat, nasty motherfucker Dirty. You know the drill."

Blue pulled up next to a big, black guy with dirty-looking dreads. As soon as the Caravan stopped, Dirty opened the side door and placed a shoe box inside the van. He then closed the door, pounded twice on the back of the van, and Blue drove off. Hype placed the box on top of a pound scale and wrote down the weight of the box next to the street corner before he gave Blue the cue to pop open the stash box. The stash box was installed into the floor of the van, underneath the middle row of seats. Once the door was opened, Hype placed the box inside the stash, next to three similar boxes. After shutting the stash door, he hopped back up front with Blue.

"One more stop and we can call it a day," Blue said, knowing how bad his man wanted to blow.

Blue and Hype's job was to pick up all the money from Too-reel's spots and weigh it. Since all the money in the boxes was supposed to be hundred-dollar bills, and each bill weighed a gram, that made every twenty-eight hundred dollars equal an ounce, and forty-four thousand, eight hundred dollars weighed a pound. Each box they collected weighed approximately five pounds, so Blue and Hype were in charge of a lot of money at any given time. Once Too-reel got the money, the amount was verified by money counters. Anyone who came up short was dealt with quickly and efficiently.

Blue was Too-reel's protégé. Too-reel took a liking to Blue because he was mature beyond his nineteen years, was exceedingly smart, and business wise. Blue was a slim kid and stood at an even six feet. He had a pretty good grade of hair and was considered to be a pretty boy for the way he dressed and took care of himself, even though he was midnight black in complexion.

Hype was Blue's partner in crime and closest friend. They grew up on the same street, and Blue even gave Hype the name Hype Williams because he always exaggerated when he told stories. Hype was young and wild with a medium build, light skin, and big eyes like Bernie Mac the comedian. People often referred to the pair as Night and Day.

"Happy birthday! Get up, Tammie, or you're going to sleep your entire birthday away," Tashiba said as she dove on top of her best friend and kissed her on the forehead.

"Thank you, Tashiba," Tammie replied in a groggy voice. "What time is it?" She yawned as she stretched out her arms and legs.

"Cover your mouth! Your breath is kicking, bitch! I see why Too-reel won't fuck with you now. If he's got to smell that shit in the morning, it's like waking up in the bathroom while someone is taking a shit."

"Fuck you, bitch. If it wasn't for that bitch Vanessa, I could have had him. That bitch has a hold on him."

Tammie threw the covers off and rolled out of bed. She was butt naked as she headed toward her bathroom.

Although Tashiba was "strictly dickly," she couldn't help but admire her friend's chocolate, milk brown complexion, and firm body. Her breasts sat straight up as if she were sixteen. Her ass cheeks rolled up and down with every step she took. Tammie kept her body tight by eating right and exercising. Her slanted eyes and silky, long, black hair made her look like she was mixed with Chinese.

Tammie had earned the nickname Deceive for her innocent looks, but ruthless behavior. Rumors circulated about her cutting off niggas' balls and stuffing them into their mouths before she killed them. She was one of the few females who was feared in the streets. She was also Too-reel's business partner. She was in love with him, but never expressed her feelings because of their business dealings.

"Call Beaty, my hairdresser, and let her know I'll be there in an hour or so," Deceive told Tashiba as she closed the bathroom door.

Tashiba was one of the closest people to Deceive, and one of the few people who still called her Tammie. Cinnamon brown with short hair and a round face, Tashiba was thick as a Wendy's frosty. What she lacked in breasts, she made up for with ass, hips, and thighs.

Tashiba used to drive drugs for Deceive's older brother, Bankroll, before he was murdered. Bankroll was killed when he refused to give up his jewelry to two young stick-up kids, who then shot him dead. They took his chain and watch before fleeing the scene. Six months later, while at a club, Tashiba spotted two guys in the club wearing Bankroll's jewelry and called Deceive. Deceive told her to keep them there until she got there. The bodies of the two young men were found in the women's bathroom with several gunshot wounds to the face and head. To this day, Deceive wore her brother's jewelry to send a message and to always remind her what her brother had died for.

When Bankroll died, he had most of his drugs and money stashed with Deceive. She decided she was going to take his place in the game. Since she was a female in a man's world, she had to be very fierce to earn respect. After the bodies of a few guys who had tried her surfaced with their balls severed and stuffed in their mouths, the message came through loud and clear. Even though Bankroll hadn't taught her the game, he had shown her the game. She had studied his every move when he was alive and had learned a lot. She quickly assembled a very close-knit clique of females who were now known as Eve's Garden.

As Deceive toweled off, she heard the buzzing of her doorbell. After meticulously applying her makeup, she dressed in a pair of thousand-dollar, stone-washed jeans, an orange and green Fendi sweater, and a pair of baby blue sneakers before she stepped out into her living room.

"Bitch, why didn't you call me back last night?" she asked her girl, Man.

"I was going to, but I was getting some of the best head of my life. I almost wanted to give this nigga the pussy and wife him. But that nigga was another slut with a good tongue. He don't think I know he fuck with that bitch, Sparkles, from uptown. Crab-ass nigga!" Man had just finished licking her blunt and was in the process of lighting it. "Happy birthday, though, my nigga," she said in the middle of two deep pulls from the blunt.

"Fuck that! What you got for a bitch? You're always tricking on those bum-ass niggas. I know you got your girl something." Deceive took the blunt from Man.

"Shit, you already got everything a bitch could want and need. Oh, my bad, except for a warm dick connected to a man. Let me see if I can find you a blowup doll with a heated vibrator!"

Man and Tashiba erupted into laughter.

"That shit's not funny, bitch. Plus, I'm saving myself."

"For who?" Man asked.

"Bet you I know," Tashiba said, giving Man a here-we-go-again look.

Man had a peanut butter brown complexion and was tall and slim. She was built like a supermodel and had the face to go with the body. She almost looked like Vanessa Williams, except Man's eyes were a bright caramel brown.

Many people thought Man was a lesbian because she dressed and acted like a thug. But nothing could have been further from the truth. Man had guys worshipping the ground she walked on. Most of the time, she would just get her pussy eaten, then dismiss the nigga. When she chose to give up the pussy, it was for her satisfaction only.

Man had totally flipped the script. She had guys staying home, cooking and cleaning, waiting for her to call or come by while she ran the streets. She took them shopping and all. She was known to be a hothead and kept two guns on her at all times, and a machine gun in the back of her Yukon that sat on twenty-six-inch rims.

"The party starts at eleven, so act surprised when you walk through the door. We put a lot into this one," Man told Deceive.

"Where's it at?"

"Club New York."

Chapter 2

The club was jumping as everyone awaited the birthday girl's arrival. Man, Tashiba, and Sonia had spared no expense on their boss and friend's party. Champagne was being served, along with catered food. But the ballers were still all at the bar, doing what they did. DJ Whoo-kid was on the ones and twos, mixing the latest hits. Every gold digger and baller scout made herself visible on the dance floor or close to the bar in skin-tight outfits. Everyone knew Deceive's party would not only bring out the underworld big shots but also the legitimate players as well.

Money tended to rub elbows with more money, so in some way or another, they were all a part of the same circle—guys from the block to the guys who supplied the blocks. And where there were drug dealers, there were also going to be lawyers, along with rappers, athletes, and even a few actors.

The VIP booths were all crowded, except for the Presidential Suite, which was reserved for Deceive and her party of girlfriends. Each VIP booth consisted of a king-sized bed, flat screen TV, and a private waiter. The Presidential Suite was situated above the dance floor with a balcony overlooking the entire club. It came with its own security detail and waiters, two bedrooms with flat screens, and access to cameras that led to the suite. There was also a mini-bar and Jacuzzi.

"Where the fuck is she? It's already after one," Sonia said, checking her Breitling wristwatch. Sonia had a high yellow complexion and wore her red hair, which was dyed, long and loose down her back. Her plump, sunset-pink lips and big eyes reminded people of Lisa Bonet from *The Cosby Show*. She was the oldest and wisest of the group. She did all the planning and overseeing of all legal activities, and was the closest thing to family to Deceive, next to

Tashiba.

Sonia had been Bankroll's fiancée. Although Bankroll had many females, Sonia was the one he trusted, and to who he exposed his whole business. Sonia became his third set of eyes and sixth sense. Her intuition was always flawless. When she told Bankroll to do something, and he didn't listen, he would surely regret it later. He learned quickly to take heed to her directions. Once Deceive decided to carry her brother's torch, Sonia continued her valuable position.

"You know Deceive. If it ain't about money, there ain't no rush," Man said, sipping champagne as she looked at the dance floor. Man's phone beeped and vibrated. She retrieved it from her waist and stared at the screen. "They're on their way inside right now!" she said as she flipped her phone shut and placed it back in her Evisu jeans.

Security cleared a path for Deceive and Tashiba. The crowd erupted with cheers as the music came to a stop. Everyone sang "Happy Birthday" as they strolled through the partygoers.

Deceive smiled and waved like she was a beauty queen on a parade float. The snow-white strapless D&G dress she wore stopped just above her knees and was embellished with gold trimming. The dress was custom made and had been flown in straight from Paris, arriving only an hour earlier. Deceive had accessorized the dress with knee-high, ivory, ostrich-skin boots with a solid gold and diamond buckle circling the ankles. A princess-cut diamond necklace rested flawlessly around her neck, along with matching earrings and bracelet.

Tashiba was right behind her in a cotton candy pink Christian Dior baby doll dress that stopped right above her curvaceous thighs. She was just happy that Deceive loved her party. She'd better since they had spent over a hundred and fifty thousand on this celebration.

After receiving hugs and kisses from a few acquaintances, Deceive and Tashiba made their way upstairs. The guards nodded and drooled over the two as they passed them to enter the suite. Sonia stood in front of the door with her arms crossed, her lips pouting.

"I know, I know, but I'm here now, Sonia. And I love the party, guys. Thank you!"

Sonia cracked a smile and gave her a hug. "Happy twenty-eighth birthday, baby girl."

"Thank you."

"Here you go," Man said, handing Deceive a long, gift-wrapped box.

"What is it?" Deceive's face lit up as she ripped open the present. Once she removed the lid, her smile vanished. There was a small dildo with a huge mushroom-shaped head resting in the box.

"That's for them lonely nights," Man said. All the girls folded over in laughter.

"Fuck you, Man!" Deceive said as she slipped the dildo into her purse.

"Let's celebrate!" Sonia walked over to the huge coffee table in the middle of the room and got a bottle of Ace of Spades champagne from a bucket filled with ice. When she popped the cork, it flew across the room as champagne gushed forth from the bottle like a geyser. She poured out four glasses, and they held their glasses up to toast the celebrant.

"Happy birthday to my little sister, and may you have many more." They all clinked their glasses.

Too-reel had just arrived at the party and was parked outside in a black Maybach with curtains drawn over the windows. He really didn't feel like being out tonight, but he had to show up for Deceive's party. He was deep in thought when his driver snapped him back to reality. "Sir, are you all right? We've been parked for the last ten minutes, and people are starting to stare."

"I'm straight, Mr. P. I was just thinking about something. I guess I might as well go inside, huh?"

Too-reel grabbed a huge, gift-wrapped box and exited the car before his driver could get out. Blue and Hype were waiting for him. Hype threw away a small roach after taking two last pulls and burning his fingers. They approached the side entrance of the club where fewer people were waiting. The bouncers knew who they were and stepped aside as Too-reel and his crew entered the club. The metal detector went off as soon as they all passed through it. The bouncers didn't even bother to give the men a second look.

The music blasted as they entered the club. The first thing Hype and Blue noticed were the topless waitresses serving drinks.

"Damn, do you see that shit? They done turned Deceive's party into a strip club!" Hype said as he ogled a waitress with watermelon-sized breasts. "Do you see all the bitches? They got to outnumber the niggas in here five to one. I'm going to see if a nigga can get a threesome popping off in this bitch tonight!"

"Shout out to my man Too-reel that just walked up in this bitch. This one's for you, my nigga," DJ Whoo-kid said as he put on 50's new song about getting money.

Too-reel gave a few people daps and hugs as he made his way to the VIP suite. As they climbed the stairs, he spotted his general, Ice, sitting at the bar with his arms around two females. When Ice spotted Too-reel, he left the two girls at the bar to join his team.

"What's good, my brothers?" Ice asked, a little out of breath from scaling the steps. They were just entering the suite when he caught up to them.

"Ice, who was the bitch in black just now?" Hype asked.

"Just some girl I just met. Why?"

"Nothing, I was just checking out shorty. She looks like my type."

"Nigga, all bitches are your type," Blue said.

"Happy birthday!" they all yelled as they approached Deceive and gave her a hug. Too-reel was the last one to give her a hug. He also gave her the gift he carried.

"Oh my God, thank you. What is it?"

"Why don't you open it," Too-reel replied, now sitting on the leather couch.

"Not yet. Ice, where's my gift at? You come in here all diamonded out with your Akon-looking ass. Let me see, blue diamond pinky ring, big bracelets on each hand, at least ten carats apiece, and three diamond chains—you got a pink, yellow, and blue one. And let's not forget those two big ice cube-shaped rocks in your ears. You look like a fucking rainbow, nigga. With all that ice on, I see why you don't dress up. Don't you know diamonds are a girl's best friend?"

"That's not true," Ice replied as he licked his lips, still smiling from ear to ear at Deceive.

"Get your nasty self out of my face." Deceive playfully pushed Ice in his chest. Sonia poured more glasses of champagne and gave them to the boys.

Deceive swore she saw the box Too-reel gave her move. She knew she wasn't that drunk yet. She bent down and took off the top and a black and white dotted, red-nosed puppy leaped up at her and barked. Deceive was startled and fell backward. Too-reel let out a small chuckle. Once she realized it was a puppy, she picked the dog up.

"Ooh, it's so cute. What is it, a boy or a girl?" she asked as she looked over at Too-reel.

"It's a boy. He'll be more protective that way."

"Thank you." Deceived noticed a small box hanging from the dog's collar. She took it off and opened the box. Inside was a pink diamond necklace set in eighteen-karat white gold. Her eyes lit up.

"What's this?" she asked as she held it up in the air.

All the girls gathered around her to admire the gift. She got up from the floor, walked over to Too-reel, and placed a kiss on his lips that caught him off guard. He licked his lips and tasted her strawberry lip gloss.

"I don't know about y'all, but I'm ready to party!" Deceive took her puppy with her as she and the girls left to go party. Blue and Hype followed behind them. They knew the baller scouts were out and hungry to find new talent. Ice stayed back to holler at Too-reel. He had noticed the grim look in his eyes.

"You look like you could use a drink," Ice said as he reached behind the mini bar and got a bottle of Hennessy. He cracked the seal and poured himself a glass.

"Pour me one, too," Too-reel said absently.

Ice knew something was wrong now because Too-reel rarely drank, and he noticed Too-reel had also finished his champagne. He poured another glass and handed it over before rolling up some strawberry 'dro. He then took a seat across from Too-reel, fired up his blunt, and sipped his cognac. "So, what's up?"

"I can't say right now."

"You know I'm here when you're ready."

"I know. When the time is right, I'll fill you in." That was all Ice needed to hear. He made casual conversation until his blunt went out on him. He then cuffed it and made his way downstairs to go play.

The party was in full swing as the Eve's Garden girls took to the dance floor, getting their groove on. They had many admirers as well as haters watching them from every angle. Man stood to the side, talking to a gentleman in a suit. She wasn't too big on dancing.

Not only were the gold diggers and ballers out in full effect, but so were the wolves—in particular, Cruddy and his Hyenas. They stood in the back of the party, by the wall, watching the action. They were appraising potential victims, weeding out the one-night ballers from the real high rollers. They knew to watch out for the people who only had money for this one occasion and would be broke again by the end of the night. Sure, they looked fly and were pushing something outside, but their pockets were on E.

Cruddy and his Hyenas were very dangerous, professional robbers. They were never unarmed. If they couldn't get their guns inside with them, like tonight, then they toted scalpel-sharp, custom-made, Plexiglas knives. Cruddy's group only targeted the biggest boys in the game. They were trained to distinguish cheap jewelry from the expensive stuff. And since most of the real ballers had a certain swagger to them, it was easy for Cruddy to single them out. No matter how they tried to downplay themselves by dressing simple and not wearing any jewelry, he could always tell who the important ones were by the way their peers were protective of them, as if guarding their meal ticket, which, in fact, was the case.

Cruddy's circle consisted of four of the most seductive bitches that ever lived. They worked the floor as he and his goons watched closely in the background. Sometimes, the girls would score big the first night, but most times, it took weeks, even months of planning and patience.

"I would love to fuck that bitch Deceive. Damn, that bitch's fine!" Cutter, one of Cruddy's top Hyenas, yelled over the loud music.

"Stay focused. We're not here for that," Cruddy whispered in Cutter's ear as he continued to watch one of his prey at the bar, buying one of his girls a drink. His squinting eyes always gave the impression that he was scheming on something, which he was. His broad nose began to sweat when he became angry.

Cruddy was as grimy as they came. If someone slipped, no matter how important, he would be there to get that person. To him, the bigger the fish, the bigger the rush, and the fish he had his eyes on tonight was Too-reel.

"Daddy, I think I got me a jeweler," a short, thick, golden-brown complexioned female in an aqua, baby doll Chanel dress whispered in Cruddy's ear.

"What's the face value?"

"Between his pinky ring, chain, and watch alone, he's got to be a quarter mil easy. And he doesn't come off as the type that keeps all his money in the bank."

Cruddy digested the information. "Calculated time?"

"Give me a week with him, and I'll know the date his mother conceived him."

"You have three days to convince me of an extension."

"No problem, Daddy," she whispered as she planted a kiss on his cheek, turned, and sashayed away.

Cruddy grabbed her by her wrist and pulled her back toward him. "Good job, Babydoll. Now go make Daddy proud." He slapped her on the ass as he let go of her wrist.

To the average eyes, it might have looked like a sexual advance. But to the rest of the Hyenas, that was their cue that she was on the job. One or two of the guys would follow and keep an eye on her at all times. They were called shadows. Every girl had her own shadow who followed her on jobs, just in case the mark got out of hand or, more importantly, an opportunity presented itself.

Each of his four girls was a beauty in her own way. Babydoll had that Megan Good look, big lips and all. China, a mix between Spanish and Asian, had the body of Venus, and a sensuous, exotic look. Egypt, with her rippling black hair, dark bronze complexion, and mysterious cat eyes brought to mind a feline enchantress. Last, but not least was Cocaine, one of the sexiest white girls to grace the planet. With blond hair, blue eyes, measuring in at a curvaceous thirty-four, twenty-eight, forty, Cocaine oozed sex. She had the look of a porno queen and was known as the Black man's kryptonite. Many ballers had fallen victim to her. She was like flesh-and-bone cocaine—one hit, and you were hooked.

All the girls knew to stay clear of the so-called player types who just wanted to hit and run. Unless they caught one slipping and they had exposed their hands for the taking, nothing was happening.

"Hey, watch where the fuck you're going!" a staggering drunk shouted as he bumped into Cruddy, spilling liquor on Cruddy's shirt.

Cruddy held up his hands in a surrender pose. The drunken man thought he was sorry or scared, but little did he know, Cruddy was telling his goons to be easy.

"That's what the fuck I thought," the drunk replied as he walked off, bumping into more people.

Cruddy poked Cutter in his side with his elbow. Without a word spoken, Cutter followed the guy into the men's room. When Cutter entered the restroom, he was greeted by the back of the guy's Pelle coat turning into the last stall. As Cutter approached the stall, he heard the drunk throwing up. When he got closer, he saw the door was cracked, and the guy was on his knees with his face buried in the toilet bowl. Cutter eased a knife from his pocket as he opened the stall door and slid inside. He eased the door shut without the guy noticing he was in the stall with him.

"Hey, cuz, you a'ight? Let me help you."

As the guy held his head up to look behind him, Cutter grabbed him by his chin with his palm covering his mouth. Cutter brought the knife down, stabbing the guy in the neck over and over with the other hand as he smothered him at the same time. The gagging noises the kid made sounded like he was still throwing up.

Cutter was an expert with knives. He knew which spots to hit to get the least reaction as his victim's blood leaked out. He had done fifteen years in a penitentiary and had gotten away with three murders while there.

Cutter positioned the guy's body to sit up on top of the toilet while his blood spilled out all over his clothes. He then used the roll of toilet paper to clean off his knife and his hands before stepping out of the stall. Seven other guys were in the bathroom. Three were at the urinals, while two were at the sink, washing their hands and checking themselves out in the mirror. Two more were in a stall, getting high off coke. No one seemed to notice what had just taken place.

Cutter washed his hands and exited the bathroom. He didn't bother to join Cruddy. He went straight out the front exit of the club. On his way out, he made eye contact with a thick shorty with short hair, dancing next to Deceive. She smiled at him with lust in her eyes. He smiled back but kept going.

"Flirting, are we?" Sonia asked as she caught Tashiba.

"I'm just having fun, that's all." Tashiba was feeling the dark-skinned guy with the stocky build. He looked like straight trouble to her, and that intrigued her.

"I've got to go pee. Here." Deceive handed her dog to Tashiba as she made a dash to the suite.

"Why don't you take this damn dog with you?" Tashiba yelled, but it was too late. Deceive made her way up the stairs. She was feeling really good from all the alcohol. She almost tripped over a box as she entered the suite.

"Fuck! Ooh, you're still up here. Why aren't you downstairs at the party?" she asked when she spotted Too-reel still in the same spot she'd left him two hours earlier.

"I'm good. I'm just chilling, thinking about something," he answered in his raspy voice.

"You're always thinking. It's my party. You're supposed to be having fun." Deceive walked to the bathroom and left the door open as she lifted her dress and sat to pee. "Aahh," she moaned in relief. When she finished, she wiped herself and washed her hands. She exited the bathroom, running her fingers over the necklace Too-reel had given her. "I really like my gift," she said. She went over and sat right next to him.

"I'm glad you like it."

"Are you OK?"

"I'm straight, just zoning out."

"This one's for the birthday girl, wherever you are!" Whoo-kid yelled over the microphone as Ginuwine's song "So Anxious" blared from the speakers.

"Oh, my God! That's my song. Come dance with me." She hopped to her feet, pulling Too-reel by his hand.

"Whoa, I'm not a good dancer, you know." Too-reel hesitated a little, pulling his hand back.

"Don't worry about that. Just follow my lead."

Deceive threw his hands around her back as she snuggled up against his chest and started rocking back and forth. Too-reel became aroused by her soft body pressing against his. Deceive knew exactly what she was doing when she felt Too-reel get aroused. She turned around, pressing her firm ass up on his cock while grinding. It must have been the liquor taking over because Too-reel began caressing her breasts and kissing her neck. He was driving Deceive crazy. She turned around and kissed Too-reel aggressively.

She had envisioned this moment for a long time. She pulled him toward the bed while they still kissed. She started unbuckling his pants, reaching inside to retrieve his erect dick. It was rock hard as she held it in her hand. She stroked it twice before lying back onto the bed and pulling him on top of her. He inserted himself inside her. Deceive tensed up, arching her back. After a few deep strokes, the pain was replaced by pleasure. She pulled him deeper and deeper inside her, meeting his rhythm.

As Too-reel pounded Deceive's body, he saw visions of Vanessa's face each time he looked at Deceive. The more he saw Vanessa's face, the angrier he became, and the harder he began to thrust into Deceive. He was unconscious of his actions, even as his hands wrapped around Deceive's neck and began to choke her.

"You fucking bitch! How could you do this to me!" Too-reel mumbled as he applied more pressure to Deceive's neck.

"Stop it. You're really hurting me. Stop!" Deceive tried pushing Too-reel off her, but it was useless. "Stop, stop!" She began punching Too-reel in the chest. Before she realized it, she was having a huge orgasm. She screamed from the pleasure she was experiencing. Never before had she cum like that. Her screaming snapped Too-reel out of his trance.

"Ooh, shit! I'm sorry, Deceive!" he said in a panicked voice as he jumped off her and started fixing himself. Deceive had tears rolling down her cheeks, along with a spaced-out look on her face. Too-reel kept repeating how sorry he was as he tried to straighten her clothes.

"It's OK. I'm good, thank you. I'm going to lie here for a while," she said in a zoned-out voice. She sat up and kissed Too-reel on his cheek before lying back down on the bed, curling up into the fetal position. Too-reel's worries were eased after she kissed him. He got back up and left her there.

Chapter 3

"Hello, Agent Tyson, please come in," Jerol said as he stood behind his desk and extended his hand to Vanessa. Vanessa entered and took the offered hand.

"How are you doing this morning, Christal?" Director Burgull asked as he closed the door behind her. Burgull was in his late forties. He still rocked a crew cut from his many years in the Army. He stood six-feet-four-inches, weighed two hundred and twenty-three pounds, and possessed a round face with a small chin and dark-brown eyes.

"I'm fine, director, and how are you?" Vanessa took a seat on a coffee-brown leather couch.

"You know, just another day closer to retirement," the director said as he and Jerol shared a chuckle.

"I bet you can't wait," Jerol said. "Anyway, Agent Tyson, I'm going to get straight to the point. It has come to my attention that you have filed for a transfer."

"Yes, I've completed my assignment, and the report has been filed."

"Yes, you have, Agent Tyson, and I must say, your work has been outstanding. I commend you on a job well done. That is why I need you to stay on board and finish this one out."

"What do you mean? What else is there for me to do? You guys asked me to go undercover and build a solid case, which I did. Furthermore, he knows who I am, and I would be endangering my life if I pursued this case any further." Vanessa wondered exactly where they were going with this.

"Christal, this case is very delicate, and only your soft touch can help resolve it," the director said. "I can assure you I would never jeopardize one of my field agents or any agent for that matter. You will be helping us take a lot of drugs off the streets and give the next generation a better chance. This Too-reel character can be a big help to us."

"But I have already delivered him to you guys on a silver platter. What else do you want from me?" Vanessa was trying her best to hold it together.

"I don't expect much from you, Agent Tyson," Jerol said. "Just try your hand and see what happens. Mr. Cobe has deep feelings for you, or else you wouldn't have gotten this close to him. We've been on him for almost ten years now, and you broke him in less than two years. He might be a little upset at you, but I guarantee you those feelings of love are still there. It will be up to you to get back that love. Trust me, it can be done."

"For what? What is the purpose?"

"Christal, I know this case has been very stressful and strenuous on you," Jerol said, "but I will personally recommend your promotion and help you get to wherever it is you're trying to go once this is over. All I'm asking is for you to give it a try. If he takes you back, fine. If not, you'll still get the promotion and the transfer approved."

"You still haven't told me why," she said.

"Well, Mr. Cobe is very unpredictable and smart. I need someone to keep a close eye on him."

"After what I've done to him, he'll never trust me again."

"At this point in the game, we don't need his trust. I just need to know his moves. Do what it takes to convince him you still love him. We'll give you all the space you need. The account will be the same one you've been using. The only thing you need to do is report directly to me or the director every chance you get. I don't care if it's just a text, I want to know you're safe."

Vanessa knew Jerol was feeding her bullshit. She was trapped in the middle of a scheme, like a chess game, and she was the pawn. One part of her wanted to explain herself to Too-reel, the other half wanted to run and hide, to put this all behind her.

"I will get back to Director Burgull with my answer," Vanessa said as she got up to leave.

"That's all we ask." Jerol stood and shook Vanessa's hand once more.

"I expect to hear from you soon, Christal," Burgull said as he shook Vanessa's hand firmly.

"You will, sir." Vanessa exited the office, and the door was closed behind her.

"Can she be trusted?" Jerol asked.

"She's a woman who is motivated by her emotions," Burgull said.

"That makes her predictable. She'll be calling you in two days tops."

"The lab results on her blood test came back. She's pregnant."

"That's good. I want someone on her at all times. If she takes a piss without our knowledge, she'll be charged and prosecuted. If she doesn't want to go to prison, she will do what I say. The net has been set. Now, all we've got to do is wait on her to fall."

*****

Deceive was awakened by the sound of birds chirping by her window and the beaming sunlight. She held up her arm to block the sunlight as she turned her back to the window. "Aahh!" she grumbled.

Her entire body was sore, especially between her legs. Deceive was still a little drowsy from last night's alcohol. She started wondering whether last night had really taken place. Why was Too-reel so rough during sex, but most of all, why did she enjoy it? She was turned on so much when he started choking her. As flashes of Too-reel on top of her went through her mind, she started fondling herself. She was about to really get into it when her room door swung open, and Tashiba walked in.

"I see you're alive, Ms. Thang." Tashiba took a seat on the edge of the bed.

"What time is it?"

"After one. So, are you going to tell me what happened?" Tashiba asked with one eyebrow raised.

"What are you talking about?"

"Don't play stupid with me. I'm talking about you and Too-reel last night. All of a sudden, you go upstairs and don't come back down. When I found you, your clothes were all wrinkled and smelled of sex!"

"I don't know what you're talking about, Tashiba. I don't even know what happened last night."

"So, what are you saying? He took the pussy and knocked you out? Or he knocked you out, then took the pussy?" Tashiba looked at

Deceive with a smirk on her face.

"No one did anything to me last night, so just leave me alone."

"OK, if that's how you want to play it, it's cool, but you can't hide shit from me. I've known you too long."

Rufff! Rufff! Rufff! Rufff!

Deceive's puppy ran into the room. Tashiba bent down and scooped him up. "Come here, boy. He's so cute now that I can see him good. What are you going to name him?"

"Because of the color of his eyes, I was going to name him White Lightning, but his white coat made me want to call him Powder."

"I don't like White Lightning. Let's just call him Powder. That sounds better."

"So be it. Powder it is." Deceive took the dog from Tashiba. "Damn, how did I get here?"

"You really don't remember shit, huh? When Too-reel was leaving, he told me you were upstairs sleeping, so I just let you sleep until we were leaving. You don't even remember us waking you up? That's it, no more drinking for you. So I guess you don't remember about Ice's cousin, either."

"No, what happened?"

"They found him in the bathroom, stabbed up pretty bad."

"For real?" Deceive asked with her eyes wide open. Who did it?" She was fully awake now.

"Nobody knows."

"What did Ice say?" Deceive knew Ice was going to flip out.

"He's tripping, for real. You know how that nigga gets. He already got fifty gees on any information on the killer. With that type of money being offered, it's only a matter of time before someone tells it."

"Damn, I've got to call him."

"His phone is off. I've already tried. That shit even made the news."

"What about Too-reel?"

"Why don't you call him and find out."

"I will. Later, though. Right now, I'm hungry as fuck, and I need to go soak in the tub." Deceive got out of bed, still wearing last night's outfit.

"I wonder why you've got to go soak." Tashiba gave Deceive a suspicious look. Deceive just smiled at her.

"I don't kiss and tell."

*****

"It was nice meeting you, Jerry." Babydoll kissed her date on his forehead.

Jerry was lying butt naked on his bed, his hands and feet tied to each of the bed's four posts. Tears streamed down both sides of his petrified face as he watched his date and her two accomplices walk off with his father's diamonds and a little over one hundred and fifty thousand dollars in cash. What was he going to tell his father? The diamonds and money couldn't be reported to the police because they were obtained illegally. How could he have been so stupid to open up the safe in front of the strange girl? He was just trying to impress her so she would like him. He had done this many times and had gotten sex from women who thought he was wealthy.

It didn't take Babydoll long to put her plan into action once she saw what she needed to see. She seduced the young man with her luscious body and gave him the best blow job he had ever received in his short-lived life. She then convinced him to let her tie him up and ride him like the cowgirl she was. He loved the sound of it and was game.

After texting her shadow with the details of where she was, Babydoll played with Jerry's dick until her accomplices showed up at the doorstep. She let them in as if the house belonged to her. They then did a thorough search of the house but didn't recover anything else except what was in the safe.

Jerry knew he couldn't tell his father exactly what had taken place. He laid there humiliated as he thought about what he was going to say once they found him in this position.

Vanessa pulled up to a ranch-style house. She spotted Too-reel's truck parked a few houses down. She knew this was the one place she would find him: his mother's house. She had really gotten to know him over the past two years. This was where he went to clear his head and get a home-cooked meal. At the moment, Vanessa felt awful about exploiting and using the most intimate and personal things against him, but she had never expected to fall in love with him.

Vanessa parked and exited her car. She took two deep breaths before approaching the front door and ringing the bell. What was only thirty to forty seconds seemed like hours to Vanessa before someone answered the door. The front door opened slowly. Ms. Cobe stood on the other side in a sky-blue sweatshirt, glasses, and rollers in her hair, covered by a hairnet. She was a short, stocky woman with huge breasts. At fifty-two, her skin was still smooth. Vanessa and Ms. Cobe stood there, looking at each other, both not uttering a word. Vanessa's eyes said it all.

"He's in the basement."

"Thank you." Vanessa stepped inside and headed downstairs.

"Who is it, Ma?" Too-reel asked when he heard the footsteps coming down the stairs. When Vanessa entered the room, his face turned into a frown as an inferno ignited in his eyes.

"Please let me explain!" Vanessa pleaded as she stopped at the doorway.

"Explain what? How you're a cop! If you don't have an arrest warrant, I suggest you leave. You're not welcome here."

"I wanted to tell you, but I was scared. I didn't mean to hurt you like this." Tears started to flow down Vanessa's face as she spoke. "You've got to believe me, Terell, I swear."

"Don't you ever call me by that name again!" Too-reel walked toward Vanessa with his fist clenched, fire raging in his eyes. Vanessa closed her eyes, anticipating a blow.

"I started out trying to get to you because that was my job. I didn't expect to fall in love with you. It was out of my hands. I tried to get them to pull me out, but they wouldn't. I tried, I tried."

"Well, I guess your mission is complete. You should get a medal or some kind of award. You got me." Too-reel started clapping. "The great Too-reel taken down by Agent Vanessa, or is that even your real name?"

"No, it's Christal Tyson." Vanessa opened her eyes, looking at the floor as she held her head down. Too-reel was quiet for a few seconds.

"Well, you sure had me fooled, Ms. Vanessa, Christal, or whoever the fuck you are."

"The only thing I lied about was my name and occupation. But everything else is true. I do love you and still want to be with you, that's why—" Vanessa tried to touch his face when he backed up.

"Be with me! How can I be with you after what you have done? You know what I stand for, you know the people I love, and you used them against me. You made them turn me! My mother!"

"I swear I didn't know they were going to go after your mother. I would have never done it if I had known. That's the reason I'm here now, without their knowledge, trying to make things right. They want me to try to stay close to you."

"So that's the real reason you're here?"

"No, I'm here because I love you and I'm sorry. I swear I will never lie to you again. I need you. We need you."

"We? Who's we? You and the FBI?"

"No, me and your child. I'm pregnant."

"Whose is it, or is that the truth?"

"I deserve that, but I am pregnant, and it's yours." Vanessa looked Too-reel in his eyes for the first time.

"I don't believe shit you say. And I don't want no fucking kids from no trifling bitch like you anyway." Those words cut through Vanessa, especially when she knew all he wanted was to have a kid by her one day.

"I know you don't mean that. I know you. I messed up, yes, but I'm not going to keep throwing myself at you. If I don't hear from you in the next two days, I'm going to have an abortion and leave. Please don't let it end like this. I truly do love you, and I'm sorry."

Vanessa turned and ran upstairs with more tears streaming down her face. Too-reel listened to her footsteps as they ran across the living room floor and out the front door.

"Pregnant," he said to himself. Oh, how long he had wanted a child but was afraid to bring one into the world because of the lifestyle he led. A little son or daughter—it didn't really matter to him. He would never do them like his father had done him and his mother. A kid might be just what he needed to bring some calm into his life.

Too-reel's thoughts were interrupted by more footsteps coming down the stairs. He knew this time, they were his mother's. She entered the room and approached him. He knew what she was about to say.

"Now, normally, I wouldn't get into your business, but seems to me it's too late for that. I want you to be easy on that girl. I don't know what she has done, and I don't want to know. But one thing I do know is that girl's deeply in love with you. And she's in a lot of pain on the inside. We all make mistakes, but that is all a part of life.

The eyes don't lie, Terell. Don't let your pride control you for the rest of your life or you're going to be one cold and lonely person. That's all I have to say. Your dinner's ready." Ms. Cobe then exited the room as calmly as she had entered.

"I'll be up, Ma." Too-reel knew in his heart he really did love Vanessa, but how could he trust her again? Look at what she had helped them do to him. And those bastards had still sent her back? They must know how he felt.

So they want to play dirty, huh? Well, let's play, Too-reel thought as he exited the basement to go upstairs.

Chapter 4

Director Burgull exited his car and took a few steps toward his second house. He instantly noticed something was out of place. His years of working as a government agent had enhanced his observation skills. The first thing he noticed was that the latch on his front gate was unhinged, and one of his garbage cans was knocked over. He scanned the area as he ascended his porch steps. When he saw his front door ajar, he drew his pistol from his shoulder holster as he leaned to the side of the door. He used his leg to push the door open before he peered inside. Burgull proceeded to enter the house with caution.

As far as the eye could see, the place had been ransacked. Burgull kept his back to the wall as he made his way toward the living room. His police instincts told him that whoever did this was long gone, but he still kept his gun out as he continued to check out the rest of the house. When he got to his bedroom, he saw his son tied to the bed, naked.

"Jerry! What happened to you?" He ran to his son and began to untie him.

"Dad, I'm so glad to see you!" Jerry started to cry. "They were going to kill me. They said they would kill me! I didn't have any choice." Jerry's wrists and ankles were red and swollen from trying to free himself.

"Take it easy, son. Let's get you free first." Although Burgull appeared calm, he was filled with rage. *Who did this? Don't they know who I am? Somebody is going to pay for this*, he thought as he finished untying his son.

Jerry sat up and hugged his father, sobbing at the same time. "I'm sorry, Dad. I'm sorry," was all he could say.

"How long have you been like this?"

"Since . . . Sunday morning." It was now Tuesday afternoon.

Burgull had been gone from his hideaway house he normally brought his other women to. He only allowed his son to know where the house was, and he was selective of the few women he allowed to enter the home.

"No wonder your mother kept calling me. Who did this to you?"

"I . . . I don't know. I was ambushed outside by three Black guys. They forced me into the house."

"Some niggers did this to you?"

"Yeah." For some reason, Burgull didn't believe his son.

"What did they take?"

"Everything that was inside the safe." Jerry held his head down and started crying again.

"Don't worry about it, son. The main thing is that you're all right. Why don't you go get dressed? Then we can get you something to eat and clean up around here."

"OK, Dad."

Jerry grabbed his son's clothes off the floor and walked to the bathroom. Since the money and jewelry were stolen from one of his police cases, he wasn't too upset, but he still wanted to know who was responsible for this. It wasn't likely that some regular Black kids would be hanging around this part of town. And second, everyone knew he worked for the FBI.

Burgull walked to the open safe and stuck his hand inside. He felt around until he found what he was looking for. It was a very small camera that was set to start recording any time the safe was opened. The bathroom door opened and Jerry came out fully dressed with his face washed. Burgull hid the camera behind his back.

"How about something to eat? You can tell me everything that took place then," Burgull said.

"OK, Dad."

"Daddy, can I keep this?" Babydoll asked as she held up the diamond-studded chain.

"Long as you know it's going to affect your cash out." Cruddy sat at the head of a long, glass table laden with the cash and jewelry Babydoll had scored. Babydoll didn't really care about the cash, she just really liked the chain.

"Thank you, Daddy." She kissed Cruddy on the cheek.

"Wolf, I need you and Bangout to take these down to Tito. Tell him I want fifty for the watch, the diamonds, and the rest of the jewels. I want them to be put toward that other thing. He'll know exactly what I'm talking about. Let him know I'll be down there myself this weekend to see him. You and Bangout split the thirty gees he's going to give you." Cruddy handed Wolf a purple suede pouch that contained the jewelry.

Cruddy had a fencer who took all their stolen jewelry. Tito was a jeweler who had his own shop in the diamond district of Manhattan, and he did a lot of business with the famous Jacob. Tito would take the diamonds out of the jewelry, melt down the gold and platinum, and create new jewelry. Then he would pass them on to Jacob, who would later sell them to all the rappers and drug dealers who could afford them.

As Wolf and Bangout were leaving the condo, in strolled Cocaine with two handfuls of Gucci shopping bags. She walked into the living room with the plush white carpet and French-designed leather couches and dropped her bags. She then took off her Gucci high heels before walking over to Cruddy and kissing him on his cheek. Her feet left footprints in the thick carpet.

"Hello, Daddy," she whispered seductively in his ear before walking over to Babydoll and placing a kiss on her lips. Cocaine was all smiles, which either meant she had caught a victim or had good news about one.

"Somebody's been tricking," Babydoll said as she glanced over at all the shopping bags.

"You know how it is. One sniff of me and they're hooked. This trick can't get enough of me. I just met him, and already, he's asking me to marry him, telling me how he has got major paper, and he's about to give up the game so we can run off together and live happily ever after."

"Cut the bullshit and fill me in," Cruddy said. He hated to be kept in suspense.

"This trick got drunk and started telling me how he's connected with Too-reel. He's supposed to be one of the five deadly venoms. He controls the Queens section from Ozone to Springfield. He said every week, some young kids come by and pick up the take in a Caravan, not only from his spot but four others, too. He says that most of the time, he's the last stop before they head back to Brooklyn. Daddy, it's got to be a lot of money in that van. This trick just met me, and he already spent at least twenty-five grand on me today alone. I haven't even breathed on his dick yet."

Cruddy let the information formulate in his head before speaking. After two minutes of silence, he cracked a devious smile.

"I want you to juice this guy for all the information he's got on Too-reel. I don't care if you've got to suck it out of his asshole!"

"And you know I will if I have to, Daddy."

"That's what I like to hear." As Cruddy thought about finally robbing Too-reel, he felt a rush building up inside him and inside his pants also. "Babydoll, come over here and make me feel good. Cocaine, go get the toys. I feel like watching a show today."

Babydoll was oh so happy to oblige. She dropped to her knees and crawled underneath the glass table until she reached Cruddy's crotch. She pulled out his erect dick and watched as it popped straight out into her face. Cruddy closed his eyes as his head tilted backward. This was not an act of pleasure for Cruddy. This was his way of meditating. He had learned to discipline himself, separating his inner thoughts from his physical urges.

Son to a small-time pimp, Cruddy's upbringing was more of a crash course in psychology. Along with being raised in the infamous Eden Wald Housing Projects in The Bronx, New York, his thinking capacity was matched with the aggression of a wolverine.

Because of his dark complexion and fragile frame, he was always the target for people to vent their anger. The outcome was usually bloody. While doing a two-year stretch on Rikers Island for an assault, he used a razor blade he had concealed in the corner of his mouth to slash a guy in the face who was four times his size. The guy still managed to knock Cruddy out. An older prisoner ended up telling Cruddy what had happened, and he advised Cruddy to build his weight up.

By the time Cruddy left prison, he'd put on fifty pounds of solid muscle. At five-feet-eight and one hundred and ninety pounds, his physical assets now matched his aggression.

Always the thinker, after returning to his neighborhood and studying the cycle of the drug game and its players, Cruddy decided hustling wasn't for him. The consequences and pressure were too costly versus the benefits. It seemed much easier just taking the money others earned. Drama was never an issue for Cruddy, but he needed a more subtle approach than gunplay in broad daylight. It wasn't until meeting Babydoll that his plot was formalized.

Babydoll was Cruddy's first girl. He met her at a strip club when she was working. Babydoll's first love was doing life in prison for robbery and murder. Babydoll had seen something in Cruddy's eyes that drew her to him. The first night they met, they exchanged numbers. She called at three AM, telling him where she was, who she was with, and what was at the location. The robbery was practically gift-wrapped and handed to him. It was some random hustler who had picked her up at the club, but Cruddy never questioned Babydoll.

In the months that followed, he conquered her mind and body. Babydoll helped him lure his victims, and once under her trance, some of the victims would wake up the following day, tied up, while others never woke up at all.

Cruddy always kept in mind what his father had told him at the tender age of twelve: "Son, there's a few rules to the pimp game that you can apply to everyday life. I like to call it pimp-tuition, which means to have quick insight. Pimps have to think on their feet. What you say will get them to pay. You dig? You have to take the E off emotion and keep it moving. Squares get caught up in their feelings. Live off pimp principles. Bitches will pay for your company if you put some value in your time. Time is money. Never have sex for sport. If you apply this game, bitches will invest their money. And if you live off pimp principles, they have no choice but to follow their money."

Putting his father's advice into action, Cruddy was able to obtain China and Egypt. And Babydoll brought Cocaine into the picture. She met Cocaine at an upscale gentleman's club. Cruddy used his reputation and promise of riches to persuade Cutter, Bangout, Wolf, and D-Range, who were all out of prison and down on their luck, to do his bidding. He provided them with plush apartments, luxury cars, nice clothes, and, most of all, he put money in their pockets. With his four beauties and his four gunners, nothing seemed to be out of reach for Cruddy.

Cruddy looked at the clock on his living room wall and saw that it was twelve-thirty-five. Egypt and China would be there in the next fifteen minutes. *They can join the show*, he thought as he leaned his head back and closed his eyes.

*****

Too-reel sat peacefully inside his condo while incense wafted through the air. He was executing moves in his head as if he was playing a game of chess. He was about to sacrifice his queen to checkmate the king. He could see the move clearly, but when it came time to execute his move, he was stuck. He couldn't give up his queen.

Too-reel was snapped out of his thoughts by the ringing of his cell phone. He was about to turn it off when he saw the caller ID.

"Yo, what's good, Pockets?"

"That nigga Grimy was just around here trying to get something to eat. I told him to holler back at me later. I knew you was trying to catch up with him, so I gave you a call."

Pockets had just given Too-reel an idea about how to kill two birds with one stone. Grimy had robbed one of his workers and gotten away with a hundred thousand just last week. But like most stick-up kids, the money didn't last long because they didn't value it. It was easy come, easy go for most of them. Now, Grimy was trying to get his hustle on.

Niggas in the hood were backward like that. They could rob a million bucks and be broke the following day. Some would even try to hustle, but when it came time for them to re-up, nobody would serve them because of their history. There were even guys who would rob other guys from the same neighborhood they lived in and would stay out in the open like nothing occurred until they got killed. Most robbers seemed like they never planned further than getting the money. Too-reel had to laugh at some people's stupidity.

"Check this out," Too-reel said. "You know how that nigga gets down? I want you to hit him back and let him know you'll be around in the next hour. By then, I should be in hand's reach. I don't care what he wants, give it to him. If he pays you, good. If not, don't worry about it. I got you."

"That's what's up. Hit me back when you're ready."

"I'll be ready in the next two hours. That will give me plenty of time without rushing."

"One."

Too-reel clicked off his phone and retrieved a white card from the inside pocket of his jacket. He looked at the number and punched it. After three rings, the call was answered.

"Highmon speaking."

"Let's get this thing over with."

Jerol cracked a smile, but so did Too-reel. Since Too-reel planned to kill Grimy anyway, he decided to feed him to the lions to buy some more time with the Feds.

Within an hour and a half, Jerol had a unit positioned at the location Too-reel had given him. Too-reel was parked across the street from Pockets' building in a rusty-brown Oldsmobile with tinted windows. Blue sat behind the steering wheel of the Oldsmobile. All he knew was that he was supposed to tail someone. Like a good soldier, he didn't ask any questions.

Everything was a go, and Grimy should be pulling up any minute. He was supposed to be buying nine ounces of crack cocaine. A money-green 2000 Galant with smoke-gray tinted windows pulled in front of Pockets' building and parked. Grimy hopped out of the passenger side wearing a black Rocawear hoodie covering his head as he walked inside the building.

"That's the car. When he returns, stay on their ass," Too-reel told Blue. Blue was an excellent driver. He grew up stealing cars with F.P.K. (Flatbush Pullie Kids) out of Brooklyn in the early '90s. He had acquired a skill for driving while running from the police.

Within ten minutes, Grimy had emerged from the building looking conspicuous with his hands shoved inside his hoodie's pockets. He hopped back into the waiting car, and the driver pulled off. Once they were midway down the block, Blue pulled out behind them. The Galant came to a stop at the intersection by the stop sign before making a right onto Gunhill Road. Blue wasted no time letting them put any distance between them. He pulled into traffic, cutting off two oncoming vehicles at an intersection as he turned onto Gunhill Road. The Galant was five cars ahead of them. Blue glided around a Grand Cherokee while switching lanes.

"Get closer," Too-reel said as the traffic came to a stop at a red light. Blue could see the driver of the Galant telling Grimy something while looking back through her rearview. As soon as the light changed, the Galant took off, burning tires.

"Shit!" Blue shouted as he stepped on the gas. Before he could make it across the intersection, three unmarked police cars with their lights flashing flew past him, and two more made a right turn in front of him, cutting him off. He had to slam on his brakes to avoid a collision. The unmarked cars sped up behind the Galant. Blue kept a safe distance as he followed the chase. Within a few minutes, the chase came to an end with the Galant crashing into a mailbox.

As Blue drove past the scene, the police had Grimy on the floor, face down with their knees in his back as they cuffed him. Two other narcs had the driver detained. Blood ran from her forehead. As they were pulling off, Blue and Too-reel saw one of the narcs recover a plastic bag with chunks of crack rocks inside it.

"Looks like they got to him first. We could have gotten fucked up," Blue said.

"Take the bridge back to Brooklyn." Too-reel had just initiated phase one of his plan and pushed his first pawn. *Let the games begin,* he thought.

"So, Anthony, you want to tell us where you got those pretty rocks from?" The arresting narc stood in front of Grimy with his sleeves rolled up.

"Man, fuck you!"

"Is that your final answer, asshole? This is your third possession charge. Plus, it's crack cocaine, and you had a firearm in the car with you. What, you're going to say it belongs to the girl? I'm going to cut to the chase. You were set up, and your case is already federal. I'm pretty sure you know how this works. You've been tagged. You can either help or play the tough-guy role. It doesn't make a difference to me. Someone else will play."

The first thing that came to Grimy's head was that Pockets had done this to him. How else would they have just pulled him over like that? Grimy made a vow that he was going to get Pockets back one way or another. But either way, he wasn't going to prison for anyone. "Wha' do ya want? I'm willing to do whatever it takes."

"You're making the right choice. Let me make one quick phone call." The narc smiled as he exited the room. He knew they had just turned another one.

Too-reel dropped Blue off in Brooklyn and shot downtown to Manhattan, off First Street. He pulled inside a parking garage and parked before taking the elevator to the fifteenth floor. He made his way down a spacious corridor until he reached a door marked UNIT 4. His palms started to sweat as he put the key into the door and turned the lock. Thoughts raced through his head. Always in control, his feelings were now running wild.

When he opened the door, Vanessa stood there with excitement and grief written all over her face. Her eyes were puffy and red. Too-reel could tell she had been crying. He stepped inside and closed the door. They stared at each other for two minutes.

"We need to talk," Too-reel said.

"Thank you." Vanessa hugged him as she started to cry. Too-reel was reluctant to hug her, so he just stood there until she released him. He was ready to talk, but he wasn't sure if he was ready to trust her again.

Chapter 5

Boom! Boom! Boom!

Pockets instantly knew what the loud knock was. He jumped up from the bed and started pulling on his pants and shoes.

"Baby, who's that at your door this late?" his girl Tanya asked as she rolled over, looking at Pockets as he scrambled to get dressed.

"It's the police, baby. I've got to go!"

"What did you do?" Tanya was sitting up in the bed now.

"Nothing, but I'm not waiting around to find out."

Pockets opened his bedroom window and was about to climb out onto the fire escape when he was tackled to the floor by a figure diving through the window. Three more officers came through the window, all with weapons drawn. Tanya began to scream.

"Shut the fuck up!" one of the officers yelled as he turned his machine gun on her. The other two officers helped cuff Pockets and pulled him to his feet.

"What the fuck did I do?" Pockets yelled.

"There's an arrest warrant and a search warrant out for you and your apartment," the officer who tackled him replied. A squad of police came through his front door and began to tear his apartment apart.

"For what? What the fuck is this all about?"

"You've been selling drugs from this apartment. Not only is that illegal, but you've also violated your probation." They began to walk Pockets out of the apartment. "And, you, get dressed," the officer said to Tanya. "You cannot stay here while they search. Your name isn't on the lease."

"Baby, I'll be down there," Tanya said as the officers dragged Pockets outside.

"No, just go home and wait until I call you," Pockets responded.

Pockets was taken to a private building and left inside a small room for two hours before someone came to speak to him. The same muscle head narc who had arrested Grimy entered the room with a file in his hand. He dropped it in front of Pockets, uncuffed him, and told him to read it. Pockets picked up a sheet of paper from the folder and began to read.

On the date of 2-28-10, Mr. Wilson, aka Pockets, knowingly and willingly sold 250 grams of "crack" cocaine to a C.I. The drugs were tested and confirmed to be "crack" cocaine.

The report went into more details about Pockets, but he didn't bother to read the rest. He knew there was only one person he had sold nine ounces to and that was Grimy.

As Pockets thought about his predicament some more, he began to blame Too-reel for getting him in the middle of his shit. If he wasn't doing Too-reel a favor, this wouldn't have happened.

I tried to help this nigga and got jammed up. If I'm going down, he's coming with me, he thought.

Pockets looked up at the narc named Brody. "What can I do to help myself?" he asked. Brody cracked a smile.

Agent Brody was one of Jerol's dirty agents who reported to him only. Brody stood six-feet-two with a stocky build, sandy brown hair, and ocean-blue eyes. His nose was shaped like a parrot's beak. He'd served five years in the Marines before joining the FBI.

Originally from Pilot Mountain, NC, he was assigned to New York because he'd attacked one of his cousin's shooters in a courtroom. The guy wouldn't name his other two accomplices, so the other two shooters got away scot-free. That experience was one of the main reasons Brody loved getting people, Black guys in particular, to sell out their closest friends.

"Who's your supplier?" Brody asked.

"A guy called Too-reel."

Beep! Beep! Beep!

Too-reel's phone went off, alerting him that he had a voice message.

"Who the fuck's blowing me up this time of morning?" He flipped his phone open and pressed send to call the number on the screen. After two rings, a female answered.

"Hello?"

"Who's this?" Too-reel asked.

"This is Tanya, Pockets' girl."

"What's up, Tanya? Something happen?" Too-reel could tell something was wrong by the tone of her voice.

"They came and got Pockets. They took him!" Tanya was talking fast.

"Who took him, and when?"

"The cops. They busted into his apartment and got him over an hour ago. They said they had a search warrant and an arrest warrant for him. They were all over the apartment when I left. I didn't know who else to call."

"You did the right thing. I'm going to get someone on it right away. Do you know which precinct they took him to?"

"No. They made me leave the apartment, and Pockets told me to wait until he called me."

"Don't worry about a thing, Tanya. I got this. If he calls you first, hit me back with any info. If my people find out anything, I'll give you a call at this number."

"Thank you, Too-reel. You're a good friend."

"Get some sleep, Tanya." After hanging up with Tanya, Too-reel called his bondsman and gave him the information that he knew about Pockets. Next, he left a message with his lawyer. With his bondsman on the case, he would know something within the next two hours.

Too-reel wondered what kind of situation Pockets had gotten himself into. He was one of Too-reel's childhood friends, and he was Too-reel's eyes and ears in the Bronx. Too-reel had always valued his friendship.

"Aaaahh! I told you, I don't know what you're talking about."

"Word is, you got into a scuffle with him last month," Ice said as he circled his victim, who was tied to a chair.

"That nigga was fucking my baby's mother."

"So you killed him over that bitch?" Ice sliced the kid in his face with a small knife.

"Aaahh!" The kid screamed, but in reality, he didn't feel any pain. The knife had been coated with garlic, so it numbed the wound as soon as it was open. The only reason the victim screamed was because he knew he had been cut. It was a psychological game Ice played with his victims.

"I didn't kill your cousin! I swear on my daughter's life." The kid pleaded with Ice.

"Don't say no shit like that." Ice used the knife to cut the kid's jugular veins. The kid's body began to shake as he made attempts to grab his throat, but his hands were tied down. The chair rocked to one side and almost tipped over as his body became lifeless. Ice used the kid's shirt to wipe his knife clean.

"I think he was telling the truth," Hitman said as he watched Ice pace around the body.

"He was."

"So why did you kill him?"

"Fuck it. I couldn't let him go. I don't want to be watching my back every minute."

Hitman laughed at Ice's comment. After all the people he and Ice had killed, they had to constantly watch their backs anyway. One more enemy wouldn't have mattered.

"What are you going to do with the body?"

"Put him in the trunk of his car and leave it somewhere. They'll find it."

Ice pulled a cigarette from behind his ear and lit it. He took two deep drags that brought the cigarette halfway to the filter. He was under a lot of stress from his aunt and mother to find Reggie's killer. They had constantly told him to stop taking Reggie with him. Reggie was four years younger than Ice and was already drifting toward the street life when Ice and Reggie started hanging out. Since Ice couldn't talk Reggie out of the life, he did the next best thing and tried to school him. But Reggie was a troublemaker and always caused problems, thinking that because everyone knew Ice was his cousin, no harm would come to him.

And now Reggie was dead. Ice didn't really blame himself, but he knew his mother and aunt did. He knew it was part of the game they played, so all he could do now was find out who had killed his cousin, then kill that person. Ice took one last drag off the cigarette and flicked it to the floor.

"Let's do this."

"Ayo, Too-reel."

"What do you have for me, Mickey?"

"I checked every precinct in all five boroughs for this guy, and nothing came up. I even had one of my guys on the force run his name for any new charges in the last twenty-four hours, and still nothing. It's one of two things: that isn't the name he was arrested under, or he never made it to the precinct," Mickey replied in his thick, New York–Italian accent.

Too-reel knew what Mickey was implying and thought the same thing. "Thanks a lot, Mickey. As usual, your work is very much appreciated. If I need anything else, I'll give you a call."

"No problem, guy. And, Too-reel, stay away from those fucking rat bastards. I'd hate to see a good guy like you go down behind one of these cowards."

"I'll try my best, Mickey. Once again, thanks."

"Forget about it. That's what you pay me for."

Too-reel thought for a minute. What would make Pockets fold so easy? Although Too-reel knew Mickey was probably right, he still needed proof. He dialed Tonya's number. After the fifth ring, she answered.

"Tanya?"

"Hey, Too-reel. What's up?"

"Did you hear from Pockets?"

"Yeah. He should be back soon. He called and said that there was a mix-up, and as soon as they straightened it out, they would let him go. I was just about to call you."

"I'm glad everything worked out. Tell Pockets to give me a call when he gets in."

"OK, I will." Tanya hung up.

"I told you to wait for me to call," Pockets said, standing over Tanya as she hung up the phone. "And you still went ahead and called that nigga."

"I didn't know who else to call. Plus, he's your friend!"

"I don't have any friends! It's his fault I'm in this shit in the first place."

"What shit? I thought you said it was a misunderstanding. What are you talking about?"

"Shit, nothing! Stop questioning me and go fix me something to eat." Tanya got up and walked to the kitchen, leaving Pockets alone. She didn't like the way Pockets was behaving. And she didn't like how he was talking about Too-reel, the only person who had helped him out when he came home from prison. She knew Too-reel was cold, but he didn't fuck over his friends.

Too-reel knew it was official now. If Pockets was supposed to be one of his main men and he would flip that easily, how would the rest of his organization react? This situation was opening up his mind to the game and the characteristics of the people involved.

Slowly, an idea began to form in Too-reel's mind, one he hoped would solve all his problems, or at least shed some light on the problems he needed to face.

Chapter 6

Since Too-reel knew Vanessa wanted to prove her love and loyalty to him, he decided this was the perfect time to test her. As they both laid naked in bed, he made his move.

"Vanessa, I need you to do something for me."

"Baby, I'll do anything for you." She rolled over and kissed him.

"I was hoping you would say that." He looked her dead in her eyes as he spoke. "I'm not going to hold no punches. You and I both know they're using you to keep tabs on me. You also know they are willing to sacrifice you in order to get what they want."

"I know—" Too-reel placed his index finger over her lips, stopping her from talking.

"I know that you know. But I'm going to need you to trust me, OK?" Vanessa nodded. "Good. This situation has opened my eyes to a few things, and I see I'm going to have to rethink my whole operation. Before I go any further, I need to know who in my circle I can trust, and who I have to keep closer to me. I need to know who's going to fold once the head comes down. Death is the easy way out, and these people are giving life. Who's willing to do that? Do you understand me?"

Vanessa nodded.

"OK, this is where you come in. I'm going to need you to convince your superiors to give you the resources and manpower to stage a roundup. You can make it seem like you're doing this to gain my trust again. Make sure to tell them everything I'm telling you right now. That way, they'll have no doubt you're still doing your job. Because you best believe they do know how we feel about each other. That's why they are trying to get you caught up. That way they can hold something over your head. Let them know you know I'm testing you to see how far you're willing to go."

As Too-reel spoke, she couldn't help but feel like he was telling the truth, and that he was indeed using her.

"Do you think you can pull this off?" he asked.

"I know I can," Vanessa replied with confidence. "I'm going to play along with these little boys' games, but I will not become a casualty under any circumstances."

Burgull downloaded the recordings from his mini-camera to a high-tech computer. He then watched as his son opened the safe on numerous occasions and removed jewelry. Jerry had also returned the jewels every time. He saw the faces of two females on different dates before the night of the robbery. He then watched the recording from the night of the robbery. His son opened the safe, it seemed by his own choice, and then he began to showboat and ramble on about money and things he didn't have, leaving the safe open.

A baby-faced Black female seduced his son and tied him to the bed. After his son was tied to the bed, she left the room and returned with two goons. Watching how they operated, Burgull determined they were professionals. His son might have been singled out. Although the camera was positioned at a good angle, he was only able to get a view of the female and one of the males—the one with a hairy face.

"What an idiot!" he said to himself about his son's actions. *I'm going to have to talk to him, find out where he met this female*, Burgull thought. *These guys must have a fencer if they plan to get rid of that jewelry. I'm going to have to make a few rounds on some old friends in the diamond district to see what I can come up with.*

Burgull quickly made a printout of the two perps' faces. No one made a fool of Burgull or his sons. He was going to catch this little robbery gang, no matter what he had to do.

"I will have the director give you twenty to thirty men, all under your supervision. You'll also have access to the law firm building for your interrogations. Give me two days to get the paperwork cleared, and you'll be ready to move, Agent Tyson."

"Thank you. I've got to go right now. He's been keeping tabs on my comings and goings, as well as my phone calls. He's still closed in, and I know he's only testing me right now."

"Keep up the good work, Agent Tyson," Jerol replied as Vanessa made her way out of the room to take the back exit from the house where she had met Jerol. The house was seized property that had been transformed into a lounge house for a few high-ranking officials. They would phone each other in advance anytime they wanted to use the house. Jerol walked to the window and watched as Vanessa drove off. Brody emerged from the next room.

"Why are you giving her so much leeway? She's just a rookie," Brody said.

"Never question my judgment. I'll only explain this to you once. Are you familiar with the game of chess?"

"Sure."

"Well, this is just a bigger version. Agent Tyson is just a pawn on my team, but she's his queen. He values her more, so that's a weakness. I want you to stay on top of their little house cleaning. They're going to make this easier than I thought. Have two of your cronies be part of the raid while you stay as far away as possible. If Agent Tyson doesn't know by now that you work for me, I don't want her finding out.

"On another note, that small fish your guy threw us has turned out to be more helpful than I thought he would be. We have acquired two more informants, and we're putting together a conspiracy case and possibly solving two murder cases."

"That's good to hear," Brody said. "Anyone who gives you a hard time, just send them to me. Death before dishonor, huh? I'll see if I can change their minds to live and cope with doing life."

It didn't take long for Jerol to put the paperwork together and get everything approved. Vanessa had twenty-five agents at her disposal, along with several vehicles. With the help of Too-reel, she knew where every one of his top players was located. She set up the sting so the agents would strike simultaneously, scooping up everyone at once.

The girls were the first ones to get picked up. They were all at Deceive's apartment when twelve agents stormed in. Blue and Hype were ambushed while in traffic. Since Too-reel knew Ice was unpredictable, he arranged for the agents to pick up both him and Ice in front of Ice's mother's place. That way, no casualties would occur. Ice respected his mother too much to disrespect her house.

After everyone was rounded up and brought to the law firm's building, they were kept separate. Throughout processing, Vanessa remained behind a one-way mirror. She watched as each person was interrogated, starting with Deceive. The two interrogating agents were a white male and a Black female. Once Deceive was seated, the man dropped a file on the small wooden table in front of her. They waited for Deceive to reach for the file, but she didn't budge.

"Do you think this is a game, young lady?" The agent slammed his hand down on the table in front of her face. Deceive still didn't flinch.

"Take it easy, Paul. Can't you see this is not her fault? She just got herself involved with the wrong people. It's OK, Ms. Parker, we can help you, but first, you've got to help us and answer a few questions," the female agent said as she looked at Deceive. Deceive sat still as she returned the agent's stare with one of her own.

"I know you're not innocent, Ms. Parker. Why else would they call you Deceive? Selling drugs to innocent school kids must run in your family, huh? Just like your punk brother. He got off the easy way. But not you. Oh, no, not you, missy. You're going away for a very long time," the white agent said.

Deceive glared at the agent with pure hate in her eyes. If looks could kill, he would be in a closed casket.

"Didn't think you would like that one. This is the last chance you'll get to talk to us because once the DA gets ahold of you, you'll be pissing dust before you're eligible for parole. So tell us what we want to know about your boss, Too-reel."

"Ms. Parker, please help yourself," the female agent pleaded. "All we want to know about is Mr. Cobe, and then you'll be free to go on about your business. I can personally promise you that if you cooperate, you won't do one day in jail. And we'll make sure nothing happens to you."

Deceive still didn't budge or say one word. As Vanessa watched from the next room, she couldn't help but feel a little jealous. As a woman who was in love, she could see the same emotion in Deceive's eyes. She would have rather died than turn on Too-reel. The fire in Deceive's eyes also let Vanessa know that Deceive would kill for him. But there was something else about Deceive that kept throwing her off. She was so confident, as if she knew nothing was going to happen to her. Although Vanessa had met Deceive on numerous occasions and noticed how beautiful she was, she never thought anything more about her and Too-reel. But now she had developed an instant hate toward Deceive.

"You had your chance, sweetheart," the white agent said as he pressed a button on the wall and two agents entered the room to escort Deceive out. After Deceive was gone, the two interrogators looked at the black glass and shrugged.

The rest of the girls were brought in, one by one. Tashiba played the confused, I-don't-know girl and never answered any questions.

Sonia was way too smart and experienced for them to intimidate. She knew her constitutional rights and a little about the law, thanks to previous run-ins with the Feds while she was with Bankroll. "Any questions you want to ask me, you can ask my lawyer. And I'm going to sue y'all asses for illegally detaining me," were the only words she spoke.

Man thugged it out and almost got a beat down for spitting in the female interrogator's face and taking a swing at her partner. She was then dragged out of the room and left hog-tied in a holding cell.

Blue followed after Man was taken away. Too-reel had taught him to stay cool under pressure, so threats of him being jailed for numerous years were nothing more than words falling on deaf ears. "I'm young. I can do the time," was all he said.

Hype was not the least bit scared. He'd already done time in juvie and didn't really care. Although he was aware of the severity of the present situation, he was willing to do whatever time he had to do. The code and the rules of the streets had been embedded in him, and he wouldn't break that code for anything.

When it came to Ice, the interrogation proved to be just another waste of time. Ice was a man who believed in the principle of "all or nothing." His take on life was: you live and you die. If he was with you, he was with you all the way. No half stepping on his part. He had killed so many people in his lifetime, he was just waiting for karma to return the favor. He never spoke a word to the agents.

Too-reel's group seemed to be as solid as a bar of gold, which made Vanessa feel even guiltier. Never before had she witnessed loyalty of this magnitude, and to think she was once a part of this very same circle. At that moment, she realized she might never be able to make up for her betrayal of trust. She could almost feel the torment Too-reel was dealing with whenever he looked at her.

By mid-day the next day, Too-reel had arranged for five lawyers to pick up his crew. Satisfied with the outcome of his charade, he arranged for a stretch G5 Benz wagon limo to scoop up everyone as they were released and whisk them off to the JFK airport where two private jets waited on the runway. Too-reel had left a message with the captain that he would be joining his crew later at their destination: Cabo San Lucas, Mexico.

Chapter 7

"Excuse me, Valdimire. I would like to have a word with you," Burgull said as he stood in front of the glass counter with two agents standing behind him, looking like hit men.

"Just give me a sec, would you? I'm tending to this customer," the slim, Russian man replied.

"No, I won't give you a sec. I said now!"

Valdimire called over his assistant to serve the customer while he and Burgull walked into the office near the back of the store.

"You can't keep barging in here like this and scaring away my customers. I have a business to run, you know," Valdimire said.

"Well, let's not forget why you're still here to run this business. I've got a few questions for you, then I'm out of your way." Burgull pulled out copies of the two photos from the robbery recording. "Have you seen either one of these people before?" he asked.

Valdimire looked closely at the pictures. "You know I don't deal with the younger Black crowd. They cause too much trouble. The only person that really deals with them is Jacob."

"Jacob is too established to be taking stolen jewelry from street punks. What I want to know is, who's doing his dirty work for him? Who else does he work with?"

Valdimire scratched the side of his balding hairline. "You didn't get this from me, but check a store called Precious two blocks up. The owner's name is Tito. He deals with all the Black kids. He doesn't belong among us. I'm not positive, but I think he and Jacob have something going on. Now, would you please leave before someone realizes what's going on!"

"I hope you're sending me in the right direction, for your sake. I would hate to have to come back down here. It's not going to be good." Burgull exited the store, leaving the shaken Russian to ponder his comment.

"Hola?"

"Good day, sir. I have some news for you."

"About?"

"One of your associates. The one that's so real. He's in a little jam. He hasn't revealed any of the family secrets, but they're using his mother to squeeze him."

"Who has the grip?" the man with the heavy Spanish accent asked.

"Jerol Highmon."

"That's not good, no good. I have confidence in our little friend. Although we cannot trust anyone, this is a business built from trust. I will make my decision after this weekend. If there's any change in the weather, I would like to know the forecast right away. Comprende, amigo?"

"Yes, sir." Both lines disconnected.

"Everything is already taken care of, Ice. I'm on my way." Too-reel hung up and glanced at his watch. He was in a limo, on his way to the airport to catch up with his loyal clique, who was already in the air.

"I want to thank you for what you just did, Vanessa. I really appreciate it," Too-reel said.

"I told you I'll do anything for you. I know you still don't trust me like you used to, but I will prove to you I love you and that I'm on your side." Vanessa then placed her hand on top of his.

"That's good to know." Too-reel put his hand on top of hers before rubbing her stomach over her shirt. Her pregnancy was not yet showing.

"I want to ask you something, Too-reel."

"Go ahead."

"Are you and Deceive . . . involved in any other way?"

The question threw Too-reel off. "Why do you ask that?"

"Well, when she was being questioned, she seemed a little too emotional and overprotective of you."

"So what? That's love and loyalty. Maybe you can—"

"What? Learn from her?" Vanessa looked as if she was about to cry. "I just don't want you to be disappointed by another woman. That's all."

"What are you saying? That she will crack or can be cracked?"

Too-reel asked the question, but he didn't need to listen to Vanessa's answer since he knew Deceive was built like a rock. Other than the night of her party, she had never shown any sign of weakness. More than ninety-five percent of the males in the game would have folded before she would. But a small part of him wondered if Vanessa was playing jealous games, or if there might be some truth to her concerns.

"No, I just want you to be careful. That's all." Vanessa didn't want to come off as jealous, but she feared the damage was already done.

As the limo turned onto the tarmac and pulled up next to the private jet, Too-reel said, "Well, thanks for the heads up. I should be back in three days tops. I'll give you a call once I'm back." Too-reel leaned forward and placed a kiss on Vanessa's lips. Even though the kiss was warm, she didn't feel the passion that was once there. She started to question whether she was fighting a losing battle.

"Be safe," were the last words she spoke as he left the limo and ran toward the jet.

On the drive home, Vanessa was indecisive about continuing her mission to win Too-reel back. She told the driver to wait while she ran upstairs to her apartment. She decided to pack her clothes and leave for good. But when she entered the apartment, the whole place was decorated with rose petals leading toward the bedroom. She quickly followed the trail to a big, stuffed teddy bear with a Band-Aid over his heart and a note in his hand. She rushed over to the bear and grabbed the note.

The note read: THINGS ARE ROUGH NOW, BUT WE'RE GOING TO MAKE IT THROUGH THIS. I PROMISE.

It was signed with Too-reel's actual name. The bear also had a half-heart locket around its neck. Vanessa hugged the bear as if it were Too-reel himself. She then called downstairs to the driver to let him know he could leave. Maybe there was a chance for her and Too-reel after all.

"The bird's in the air, sir."

"I want to know everything he does. I want pictures of everyone he comes in contact with. I want to know what he ate, what it tasted like, what time he took a shit, and what it smelled like. Do you understand me, agent?"

"Yes, sir."

Jerol clicked off his phone and placed it into his shirt pocket. In front of him were photographs of everyone who had been interrogated, along with their files and backgrounds. As he flipped through the pictures, he came across a familiar face.

"Look what we have here. I see you're back to your old tricks. Well, let's see if we can rekindle the magic once more," Jerol laughed.

Too-reel had just screened his team for any leaks and had overlooked one of Jerol's past informants. This was turning out better than Jerol could have ever hoped.

Chapter 8

As Director Burgull approached Tito's outlet, he spotted two guys leaving. One was the hairy-faced guy from the photo. "Thomas, do you see those two guys over there?" Burgull didn't wait for him to answer. "I want you to follow them. Do not, I repeat, do not lose them. Call me as soon as you find out anything."

"Yes, sir!" Thomas took off in the direction where the two guys were headed. He didn't want to fall too far behind. Thomas spotted the two men heading across the street. As he hurried to catch up, he bumped into a few people.

"Hey!"

"Watch where the fuck you're going, asshole!"

Thomas ignored the comments as he tried to close the gap between him and his perps. He ran down the steps leading into the subway until he was back in full view of the men. Wolf and Bangout were swiping their Metro cards at the turnstile just as Thomas caught up. They walked toward the end of the platform where they stood and waited for their train.

Ten minutes later, the number 2 train roared into the station and came to a screeching stop. As soon as the doors slid open, people poured out onto the platform.

Thomas watched as the two men got on the train. He got on two cars down. Once the doors closed and the train started moving, he made his way towards the next car.

Thomas stayed behind Wolf and Bangout as he made his way through the crowded train. When he got to the door that led to the next car, he stopped and watched as the two perps stood by the side doors, talking to one another. The train made a stop, and the doors flew open as people began to exit and enter the car. Wolf and Bangout stood to the side, allowing people to pass. Just as the doors were about to close, Wolf and Bangout dashed between the doors. Bangout's jacket got caught between the doors, but he yanked it free just as the train began moving. The doors automatically opened and then slammed shut. It was too late for Thomas to do anything. He looked through the window as the train passed Wolf and Bangout, who stared and smiled back at Thomas.

Thomas was furious; they had been on to him the whole time. Burgull was not going to like this. These guys were good.

As Thomas walked to the door they had been standing in front of, he spotted a yellow receipt on the floor. He thought he had seen something fall from the guy's jacket. Maybe he would have something to bring back to Burgull after all.

"Hey, Tito, how are you doing today?" Burgull asked.

"I'm pretty good. What about yourself?"

"Someone told me you're the guy to see. I was thinking maybe you could help me out."

"That depends on what you're talking about, my friend," Tito replied with a little skepticism. Burgull then pulled out his badge.

"First off, you're going to tell me who that guy was I just saw leaving your store, who he works for, and where I can find him." Burgull pulled out the photo of Wolf and Babydoll and slammed it down on the counter. "If you give me what I want, you'll never see me again. If you don't, I'll become a living nightmare, and you will be charged as an accessory to robbery. That could put you out of business."

"Can we have this conversation in my office?"

*****

"What do you think about her?" Too-reel asked.

"She's like a mountain. She's not budging. The girl is solid. I personally handled that situation," the voice on the other end of the phone responded.

"Thanks a lot. My lawyer will have that check for you by tomorrow."

Too-reel nodded at the flight attendant who was giving him the buckle up sign.

"You know eyes are watching, so play safe."

The line clicked off. Too-reel shut his disposable phone and placed it inside his pocket. The G4 jet was about to touch down. After landing, the plane taxied up to a huge hanger where a black limo awaited. Too-reel exited the plane and hopped straight into the back of the limo.

They drove to a resort forty-five minutes away. The limo pulled into the hotel's underground garage and parked. When Too-reel exited the limo, he was greeted by a tall, muscular Mexican. The Mexican escorted Too-reel to an elevator. Once the elevator doors closed, the Mexican inserted a passkey into a special compartment and pressed a button. The elevator then stopped at a floor that wasn't listed on the elevator panel. The door opened into the penthouse.

Too-reel exited the elevator, leaving the Mexican behind as he made his way toward two double doors. He inserted a card that had been given to him at the door and waited for the light to turn green before turning the lock. Soon, he was inside a huge office with a sweeping view of the white sandy beaches and aqua-blue water below. A short, stocky old man with a glowing bronze complexion, white hair, and a thick mustache sat behind a large oak desk. He rose, approached Too-reel, and gave him a hug and a kiss on both cheeks.

"Terell, Terell, ha, ha, ha! It's been too long, my boy."

"Yes, too long indeed, Dei'z." They released each other and looked into each other's eyes. Too-reel knew Dei'z knew what was going on. He always seemed to know everything. But Too-reel would tell him anyway.

"They're using my mother to try to turn me. This DA by the name of Jerol Highmon."

"Sí, my son. I know about your problem. He's not one to play with. He's dirty, but he won't work for me or any of my associates. He's also protected by political power. This Señor Highmon is trouble, my son. All I have to say is whatever you're doing, try not to let it get out of hand. If anyone finds out you have agreed to cooperate with the government, my hands are tied.

"I know you would never speak a word of our arrangements, that is why you're standing here right now, but in no way or form do we tolerate this type of behavior. Only because you're like my son will I let you try to fix things before you pass this on and your mama can go free. I will not question you. This will be our last meeting. Now, who's going to fill your shoes? I hope it isn't that wild-looking kid I saw arriving earlier."

"Not that one. The other one. His name is Dwayne, but we call him Blue. He's very sharp, not quite where I would want him to be, but with your guidance, he should be all right."

"I'm getting too old to still be raising kids, you know."

"This will be the last one. He will take it to the next level and branch out legally."

"You have high hopes for him, don't you?"

"He's the future."

"When the time is right, I'll meet him, but for now, you have too many eyes watching you. It's time you check into your room."

Dei'z gave Too-reel another firm hug before sending him on his way.

"Terell, clean this up. Don't let me get involved."

Too-reel knew exactly what the old man meant. It wasn't personal—just the way of business. He'd bought himself some more time. He exited the office and returned to the elevator, where the tall Mexican awaited him.

After Too-reel got to his room, he checked in with his crew and let them know they were all having dinner at eight o'clock in the dining room downstairs. It was a little after five, so that gave everyone plenty of time to get themselves together.

Around seven-forty-five, everyone was seated, drinking and chatting amongst themselves. Appetizers were ordered as more drinks came. Everyone discussed their interrogations, comparing the questions they were asked. Too-reel raised his glass and tapped on it with his fork to get everyone's attention.

"I know everyone is wondering what's going on and why we are here. Yesterday was a test to see how loyal we are to one another. They will try to divide and conquer. It's the oldest trick in the book. I never really had any doubts about where your loyalty stood. We're a tight-knit family, and family doesn't go against each other for anyone, not even to save yourself! We're as one. We eat as one, we ride as one, and we die as one. From this point on, there are going to be some changes to ensure that if one of us falls, we don't tip over the rest of us. As of today, I'm standing down, and you guys will have to run the show as if I'm gone."

Everyone's eyes lit up, wondering where Too-reel was going.

"Deceive, you'll have to pick up most of the slack," Too-reel continued. "Blue, the game's about to change pace on you. This is what I've been grooming you for. Ice, your position is the same. I suggest you take young Hype under your wing. We'll discuss that later." Two waiters approached the table carrying more drinks. Too-reel stopped talking until they placed the drinks on the table and left.

"As you all know, I was the main focus of our little run-in. It's only a matter of time before they'll return. They're putting something together. Until I can resolve these matters, I'm falling back. But, like I said, nothing will change as far as how we eat, just how we go about eating. A few precautions will be made in case we take a loss. It won't be a big one. This turn of events has brought a lot to my attention. We might be feared in these streets, but there are some things people fear more than death—life in prison."

Too-reel let what he'd said soak in before he continued.

"I brought you all here so you can relax a little before we head back to the madness of the city. If you all haven't noticed, we're being watched and followed, so try to chill, and don't do anything stupid. In the meantime, let's have some fun."

The food was just arriving when Too-reel finished his little speech. Everyone dug into their plates as they thought about the information Too-reel had just shared. Things were changing.

Chapter 9

After dinner, everyone separated to do their own thing. Ice headed to the casino with Man and Sonia. Blue and Hype weren't old enough to gamble, so they decided they were going to party with the rich white girls on spring break. They had already hooked up with two girls they had met by the pool earlier that day. Blue texted them to find out where they wanted to meet. Tashiba waited to see what Deceive was trying to get into, and Too-reel headed to his suite to think and get some much-needed rest.

"So, what do you think?" Tashiba asked Deceive as they strolled the beach.

"Something is going on that Too-reel is not telling us, or rather, me," Deceive answered.

"Why would he hold back on us? Haven't we proven our loyalty?"

"I don't think it's just that. He's been distant for the last few weeks. Something is wrong."

"Like what?"

"I don't know, but I plan to find out. We are partners in crime, after all. Why don't you join Sonia and them at the casino while I go have a talk with Too-reel? Maybe I can find out exactly what's going on."

"I wonder if it's girl trouble. I haven't seen Vanessa around lately. And you know how nosey she likes to be, always up his ass."

"I doubt it. I don't think he'd let her jeopardize his business."

Deceive had to question herself on that one. She decided she would ask him herself. She also wanted to know if the night at the club was just a moment or something else because she was truly in love with him.

The girls made it back to the hotel. Tashiba went to join Man and

Sonia while Deceive rode the elevator to Too-reel's floor. When she exited the elevator, she noticed a white male in a hotel uniform, pushing a food cart. Automatically, she knew he was an agent. Most of the other staff members were Mexicans. As she walked past him, she winked at him.

"How are you doing tonight, Officer?" she asked.

"Excuse me, ma'am?" He stopped walking.

"Oh, it's all right to say Officer, or should I refer to you as Agent? What is the name on your tag? Gomez? You don't look Mexican to me."

"I'm sorry. I don't know what you're talking about," the man replied nervously.

"Now that I think about it, I did see you at the airport, and you were sitting in the far corner while we were at dinner. Yeah, that's right, you guys are getting sloppy, man. Tighten up."

Deceive turned and walked to Too-reel's door and knocked. The waiter just stood there, looking at her before he finally boarded the elevator. After seeing it was Deceive, Too-reel opened his door and let her inside.

"I see you're a famous guy," she replied as he closed the door behind her.

"Why is that?"

"Because your fans are stalking you," she replied with a smile.

"Very funny." He smiled back, knowing what she meant.

Deceive took in the view from his room. She was able to see the surrounding mountains on this side of the hotel. The bright stars illuminated the dark sky, and the night breeze mixing with the scent of the ocean brought her a sense of calmness.

Deceive kicked off her shoes as she checked out the spacious room. The living room furniture and carpets were cream-colored, and there was a plasma TV, a few lamps and tables, and a mini-bar. The living room branched off to the kitchen, another room, and a balcony. Deceive walked up to the sliding glass door leading to the balcony and looked at the sky once more. She had never seen so many stars, nor had the moon ever looked so bright.

"It's beautiful out here," she said.

"Yes, it is." Too-reel stood next to her, taking in the view.

"Do you ever think about the future?"

"Sometimes I do, but most of the time, I tell myself that today could be my last day."

"So you don't think about having any kids or a wife? A life without looking behind you all the time?"

"How can I? Plus, I never really thought about making it out alive or free. I ain't going to lie, I thought about having a kid one day. But like I said, though."

"Well, do you ever think about leaving this life behind?"

"Then what am I going to do, work?"

"Why not? It's not like you're broke."

"Deceive, why all these strange questions? Are you thinking about pulling out?" Too-reel faced Deceive.

"That's not what I'm thinking about at all."

"Then what is it?"

"I was thinking about me and you. And what happened between us the other night. Was it real or just a one-night thing?"

Too-reel knew this was going to come up sooner or later.

"I mean, what did happen?" he asked. "We were both a little drunk, and one thing led to another. It should have never happened. We're partners, after all."

"Don't give me that bullshit! Yeah, maybe we were both tipsy, as you say, but it was still not that innocent. You knew what you were doing, and I sure as hell knew what I was doing. I've been waiting for that night to happen for a long time now."

"What do you mean, you've been waiting for that night?" Too-reel looked a little puzzled.

"Are you really that blind that you can't see I'm in love with you? I've been for the past two years now. Hell, from the first time I met you. The only reason I hid it so long was because of our business dealings and, of course, your girlfriend that seems to have your heart.

"Too-reel, I've been around you for over five years now. I've never seen you like this. I know something is wrong. Let me in."

"Now isn't the right time for all of this, Deceive. Let it go."

"No, I'm not letting it go. When is the right time?"

"I said, let it go!" Too-reel turned so his back faced Deceive.

"So you can trust me with our business, your life, and your freedom, but you won't trust me with your heart?" Deceive took two steps toward him and faced him. She rubbed her hand across his face while staring into his eyes. "I love you, and I'll never betray you." She stood on her tiptoes and kissed him on his lips. He pushed her away, but she only came back and kissed him again. This time, he embraced her and kissed her back passionately.

"Look at the two of them. I guess business does mix with pleasure," an agent said as he snapped shots of Too-reel and Deceive from the rooftop of the adjacent hotel.

"I wouldn't mind pleasuring her with my business. She's a looker for a Black woman," the waiter from the hallway said.

*****

Too-reel and Deceive stripped each other as they made their way to the bedroom. Wearing only her panties, Deceive hopped on Too-reel while he stood in the middle of the room in his boxers. She wrapped her legs around his waist and kissed him.

Too-reel spread his legs to balance their weight. Deceive used one hand to reach inside his boxers and pull out his shaft. She slid her panties to the side and impaled herself on his dick. Too-reel cupped her ass cheeks and forced her down further. At first, they were a little off rhythm, but slowly, they matched each other's pace. They both moaned and kissed aggressively. Deceive sank her nails into his back as he pumped harder. With every thrust, he pulled her down harder on his dick. Deceive felt Too-reel's dick jump inside her and hopped off.

"No, not yet. I don't want you to cum."

She took his hand and led him to the bed. They were both breathing hard. Deceive laid on her back and opened her legs as far as they would go. As Too-reel stood there, admiring her sculpted body, he thought, *Damn, I'm slipping.* Even her pubic hairs were groomed into a perfect triangle. He couldn't help but taste her.

He kneeled down in front of her, spread her lips with his fingers, and began to massage her clit with his nose and chin. He made small circles while poking the end of his nose in and out of her. Deceive started trembling as her pussy trickled juices all over Too-reel's face. She rotated her hips and squeezed her nipples. Too-reel used the tip of his tongue to lightly stroke her clitoris as he inserted his index finger inside her. She began to whine harder and buck as she reached an orgasm.

"Ooooohhh!" Deceive almost kicked Too-reel in his face. He continued to suck down her sweet nectar, sending chills up and down her spine. He got so turned on to see her react like this, he was ready for his nut. He stood up and climbed on top of her while inserting himself inside her. He started out rough with deep strokes.

"Ohh, yes, yes, cum inside me," Deceive moaned as she pulled him deeper inside her.

"What are you doing?" Too-reel asked, still not missing a stroke as she placed his arms around her neck.

"I want you to choke me like you did the first time we fucked."

"Are you crazy? I can't do that."

"I like it. Please do it. It makes me cum." Deceive still had his arms around her neck. He applied a little pressure. "Harder, harder," she said.

Too-reel began to think about his father abandoning him and his mother and added more pressure, fucking Deceive harder. He thought about Jerol sending his mother to prison. Before he knew it, Deceive gagged for air as he slammed his dick in and out of her. He finally released inside her and loosened his grip around her neck. He then rolled over and collapsed next to her, sweat pouring from his body, still breathing hard. Deceive seemed to be having an out-of-body experience as she stared at the ceiling in silence.

Chapter 10

"He didn't look like any regular police officer to me," Bangout said.

"I think he was a Fed. I first noticed him when we were in the subway, but I think he followed us from Tito's," Wolf stated.

Cruddy took in everything his soldiers were telling him. What would make the Feds want to follow him or any of his guys? They only robbed dealers. And even if it was connected to a murder case, what would tie them in?

"Tito!" he said. "Let me use your burnout, Wolf."

Wolf handed Cruddy his cell phone. Cruddy dialed Tito's number and waited as the phone rang. "Yo, Tito. What's up? What do you think, pretty, huh?"

"These are very good. Where did you get these jewels from? I already have a buyer. I should have your money by tomorrow. I want to talk to you about something personal, so can you come pick up the money? How about seven-thirty? Is that good for you?"

"Not tomorrow. How about the day after? I've got to go see my sister and lend her some cash. I'll be by your place after that."

"Why don't you just call me and let me know when you're on your way, and we'll meet by the park down the block."

"I got you. See you then." Cruddy clicked off. "That bitch-ass nigga is trying to set me up!"

"How you know?" Wolf asked.

"First off, he was talking reckless, asking me where I got the shit from. He never does that. Then he wanted me to pick up the money, but not at the store; down the block by the park."

"As scary as that nigga be, he's talking about meeting in public?" Bangout asked.

"Exactly. When have any of us met him outside of his store to pick up money?" Cruddy looked at his men. "I want Egypt and China to stake out his shop and take pictures of anyone he talks to. Tell them to drop what they're doing and get down there now. I'm going to have Cutter meet them there. He can spot an agent from a block away. I want to know who he's been talking to, and how much info they got on us."

As soon as Tito hung up with Cruddy, he placed a call to Burgull.

"Burgull speaking."

"Hello, hello."

"Yeah, who's this?"

"Tito. I just got off the phone with the head guy I was telling you about. He's supposed to meet me Wednesday by the park down the block."

"That's very good, Tito. I'll be dropping by to see you so we can prep you and go over some things. Like I said earlier, the sooner this is over, the sooner we'll be out of your way." Burgull clicked off his phone.

"You're lucky, Thomas. That was the store owner, and he just arranged for them to meet him in two days. It might be a long shot, but check that receipt for prints and see what you come up with. And please try not to get lost on this one. Maloy, Newkirk, you guys come with me."

As Cutter stood across the street, getting a hot dog, he spotted a black GMC Yukon pulling up to a parked car, double parking. Two white males exited the truck. From their attire, Cutter knew they were Feds. He watched them enter Tito's store before he texted China and Egypt, who were already in the store browsing when the two agents walked in. Tito greeted the agents and escorted them to his office.

"So, what did you say this guy's name was?" Maloy asked.

"I just call him Tony. That's the only name I know him by."

"He's a Black male in his late twenties, about five-eight or five-ten, two hundred pounds with a low-cut beard, right?"

"Yeah, that's about right."

"All I want you to do is meet the guy. Nothing else! We'll take it from there," Burgull said.

"I don't care. Just leave me alone once this is over."

"No problem, Tito. If he gets in contact with you again, you know what to do," Burgull said.

Burgull and Maloy turned and left the office. As they headed outside, they were stopped by two females.

"Excuse me, gentleman, would you mind taking a picture of me and my friend? We're visiting from DC," Egypt said.

"No problem at all." Burgull took the camera from China and snapped two pictures of the women.

"Can we please get one with both of y'all in it? I just love me a man in a suit," China stated.

"Sure, why not."

"You first, sir," China said to Burgull. Both women stood on opposite sides of Burgull as Maloy took the shots. In one of the photos, both girls kissed Burgull on his cheeks at the same time.

"Your turn," China said to Maloy. They did the same thing with Maloy as Burgull took the pictures.

"Thank you!" the girls said at the same time as they walked off.

"No, thank you, ladies," Burgull said as they were getting back into the truck.

The two women went to a one-hour photo shop and got the pictures developed. Cruddy then had the girls drop off the pictures to his cousin, who worked at the Twenty-third Precinct in the narcotics division. Cruddy needed to find out who the men in the pictures were as soon as possible.

Tito pulled his pearl white Mercedes Benz 400e into the empty parking space by the small church across the street from the 40s projects off Guy Brower Boulevard. He looked through his tinted windows at the group of guys standing across the street on the corner, looking in his direction like they were scheming. Tito really hated coming to this part of Queens. Although he dealt with a lot of street guys in his business, if he wasn't taking their money, he didn't want to be around them.

Tito dipped into his inside jacket pocket and retrieved a small plastic bag containing a white, powdery substance. He opened the bag, stuck a small straw inside it, and took a couple of sniffs in each nostril. He then stuck his index finger in the bag before sticking his finger in his mouth and rubbing it across his gums. After checking his nose in the rearview mirror, making sure his face was straight, he exited the car and locked all the doors, using the alarm on his key chain.

He walked a short distance to a rundown, faded, sky-blue

wooden house with rusted gates surrounding the cluttered front yard. The front gate dragged on the concrete as Tito pushed it open and closed it behind him.

The front door to the house opened, making a creaking sound like a haunted house would. A butter pecan Hispanic girl stood in the doorway in a tight-fitting tank top with her nipples poking through. She had on an even tighter pair of gray gym shorts, leaving nothing to the imagination. Her hair was braided into a long pigtail. Tito walked past the girl and into the house as she quickly closed the door behind him.

"Shhh, my grandmother is sleeping. Let's go to the basement!" she whispered to Tito as she led him to a small, dingy basement. The basement floor was covered with a worn, stained carpet that looked like it used to be a cream color. Two old couches and a loveseat, along with one of those old, floor-model TVs filled the room. Tito frowned as he took off his blazer and placed it in the spot where he was about to sit on the couch.

"Would you like something to drink?" the young girl asked. Tito had met her one night at a ghetto strip club. She couldn't be any older than eighteen or nineteen, if that old, and she was already turned all the way out.

"No thanks, Jasmin. Let's just make this quick. I have somewhere to be soon," he lied.

"Well, you know what I like, papi."

"Of course I do."

Tito pulled out the small bag of powder. He took out a hundred-dollar bill and folded it the long way a few times before he sprinkled some of the powder onto it. He used the same straw and took two bumps before passing the money with the powder on it, along with the straw to Jasmin. She greedily took it and did the same thing. After a few more hits of the powder, she was ready to go to work. Jasmin walked over to Tito, kneeled between his legs, and unzipped his pants. She reached inside his boxers and retrieved his erect penis. She hungrily swallowed his dick and began to slob him down. As her head bobbed up and down, she made slurping sounds and moans. Tito closed his eyes and let his head fall all the way back as he placed his palm on top of Jasmin's head.

After five minutes of receiving head, Tito was ready to fuck. He pushed Jasmin's face away from his crotch. She knew what he wanted next. She rose to her feet and peeled off her gym shorts.

Tito fumbled in his pocket to find his condom. As he was opening the pack and getting ready to put it over his dick, Jasmin put on a little show, twirling and grinding inches away from his face. He admired her young body, the way her breasts stood straight up, and her ass and abs were so tight and firm. Once the condom was on, he pulled her down on top of him. As she straddled him, she guided his dick inside her wet pussy. She started off by bouncing on Tito's dick like a pogo stick. Tito wrapped his arms around her waist, palming her ass cheeks and spreading them open as he slid his index finger into her asshole. Jasmin pulled Tito's head toward her and stuck one breast into his mouth. Tito sucked like a hungry newborn.

He felt like he was in heaven as he shot off a load inside the condom. Jasmin continued to prance on top of his dick until it became soft and he withdrew it from her.

"Ahh, baby, I was just getting started," Jasmin complained.

"Maybe next time, sweetheart."

Tito pushed her off him and took off the condom.

"Throw this away for me."

Jasmin took the condom, walked to the bathroom, and flushed it. When she walked back, Tito was fixing himself. After straightening his pants, he put on his blazer. He dug into his pocket, took out some more money, and placed it next to the hundred-dollar bill and the remainder of the powder.

"Why don't you come and let me out?" he asked. Jasmin escorted him back upstairs to the front door. "I'll give you a call," Tito said as he walked off.

"No, you won't," Jasmin said as she closed the door.

Tito walked to his car in a hurry. As he looked around, he didn't see the guys who were standing on the corner when he arrived. As he approached his car, he hit the alarm button, opening all doors. He got in and closed the door, locking the locks at the same time. As he was sticking the key into the ignition, he looked in his rearview mirror and saw two eyes looking back at him. He tried to turn around but was grabbed around his neck as something sharp was stuck into his side.

"So that's how you want to play, huh? You trying to set me up?" Cruddy asked through clenched teeth.

"No, I would never do anything like that." Tito felt something pierce his side again. "Ahh."

"Don't lie to me. I know!" Cruddy whispered in his ear.

"I didn't have any choice! They were going to shut me down and lock me up. You know how it is."

"Yeah, I know how it is."

"It wasn't my fault. It was those jewels you sent me. You're the one who made it hot, not me."

"No, you became hot when you decided you were going to cooperate. Bad choice. What did you tell them?"

"Nothing. They just wanted me to get you to come see me. They wanted to talk to you. That's all they said, I swear."

Cruddy put more pressure on Tito's neck. "Speak to me about what?"

"The jewels. They didn't say exactly. They just showed me a picture of your guy Wolf and some girl."

"So where are the jewels?"

"They got them!" Tito lied.

"What are the names of the agents?"

"It was mainly one guy that did most of the talking. Burgull."

"Where's his card? I know he left you with one."

"It's in my wallet. Let me get it for you."

"No, that won't be necessary."

Cruddy stabbed Tito over thirty times in his side while choking the air from him. After Tito was dead, Cruddy reclined the seat so Tito's head didn't fall onto the steering wheel and cause the horn to go off. He took Tito's wallet and got Burgull's card and anything else of value before exiting the car.

Cruddy disappeared into the night as the crackheads and street scavengers came out from the dark and started stripping down the car, piece by piece. By the next morning, the only thing that would be left on the car would be the steering wheel and the seat where Tito lay dead. And no one would have seen a thing.

Chapter 11

Too-reel and his squad had just arrived back in town. Everyone had instructions on what to do, so they went their separate ways.

Sonia pulled up in front of her house that Bankroll had brought her in the Springfield area of Queens. The driver of the black Lincoln Town Car got out and retrieved Sonia's small suitcase from the trunk. He placed it in front of the door before walking back to the car. Sonia gave him a fifty-dollar bill. "Keep the change," she said.

"Thank you, ma'am," the driver replied before getting back into the car and pulling off.

Sonia was putting her key into her front door when a black-on-black Yukon Suburban with tinted windows pulled up in front of her house. The passenger side door flew open, along with the driver's side as two white males in black suits hopped out. They looked as if they worked for MIB or the Secret Service with their earpieces and black shades.

"Excuse me, ma'am, but there's someone who wishes to see you," the passenger said as he approached Sonia.

"Not this bullshit again. Look, if you're not here to arrest me, then you guys will have to talk to my lawyer." Sonia pulled out her cell and started to dial her lawyer's number.

"Sonia Peterson, please hang up that phone and come have a seat." The back window on the SUV rolled down halfway before rolling back up. Sonia knew exactly who that voice belonged to. How could she forget it? It sent chills down her spine.

Her legs almost gave out as she began walking toward the truck. *What does he want after all these years?* she wondered. The back door was held open for her as she got inside. "What the hell do you want? I have nothing to say to you!" she said as soon as the door closed.

"Oh, on the contrary. You have a lot to say to me."

"No, I don't. I did what I had to do over five years ago. Now leave me alone."

"It doesn't work like that, my dear. Didn't Bankroll explain it to you? What did you think, that it would just be over for you because he died?"

"No more, Jerol. I'm through!"

"No, you're through when I say you're through," Jerol stated in a calm voice. "Or would you rather me tell Little Tammie that her big sister and brother have been working for the FBI? I mean, you are like sisters, right? Hmm, I don't think she'll take the news too well."

"If you ever say anything to her about our—"

"Our what? You'll do what? The way I see it, you're not in any position to be making demands or threats. This is what you're going to do. You're going to keep me up to date with all future plans of Too-reel and Little Tammie, or should I just call her Deceive? Starting with the little trip you guys just came back from."

"Cabo was nothing but a quick breather for us. Too-reel felt he was drawing attention to the rest of us. He just basically let us know he would be pulling back a little, and things were going to change."

"Like what?"

"I'm not exactly sure. Deceive hasn't told us anything new yet."

"As soon as you know, I want to know within the hour. My numbers are still the same, but just in case you forgot, they're here." Jerol handed Sonia a card with three numbers on it. "I will be expecting to hear from you soon. You can go now."

Sonia stared at Jerol for a full minute before she exited the truck. The driver and passenger got back inside and pulled off.

Sonia scanned the area to make sure no one had seen what had just taken place. She thought her days of being blackmailed for her freedom were long gone. She never expected it to catch back up to her like this. As much as Deceive looked up to her and thought the world of her brother, this would crush her heart if she found out the things she and Bankroll had done to stay afloat on the streets.

Deceive was so caught up on the so-called codes of the streets, death-before-dishonor lifestyle, she would never understand what was really going on in these streets. Deceive was that way before she had met Too-reel, and she would probably want to kill Sonia if she ever found out.

Sonia was stuck. She couldn't tell Deceive, and she couldn't let her find out like this. Sonia picked up her suitcase and pushed her door open. She shed a few tears as she closed the door behind her, trying to figure out how her life had come to this.

"Man, this motherfucker's a director. What the fuck is he doing investigating us? He must have some special interest in this case," Cruddy said, pacing in his living room.

"From what D said, this guy is supposed to be retiring soon. He should be behind a desk or something, shouldn't he?" Cutter asked as he moved out of the way of Wolf and Bangout as they hoisted the leather couch. Cruddy had decided to move until he found out just how much Burgull knew about him.

"This piece of shit Tito still owes me a hundred gees. I'm going to have to tell Cocaine to speed things up with this guy. After we hit Too-reel, we should have enough to start over somewhere else."

"Where do you have in mind?" Cutter asked.

"I was thinking ATL, or maybe Miami. We should make a killing in the South. After that, we'll hit up the West Coast."

"Hell yeah, I'm with that."

"But before we go, I want this guy put to rest. I don't need no super cop on my trail. Have Bangout and Wolf . . . No, Wolf is too hot. Let Bangout and Egypt be this guy's shadow. I want to know where he stays, where he eats, the whole nine yards. I know he's used to following people, but let's see how he handles being followed and watched. His days are numbered."

When Too-reel got home, he received a surprising message from his mother about Jeff, his old mentor. Jeff had been transferred from the ADX supermax prison in Florence, Colorado, to Allenwood Medium in Pennsylvania. Jeff had received double life, and because of his influence, he was sent away to ADX where he wasn't to be in physical contact with anyone. Now that Jeff was at a low, Too-reel would be able to visit him. He waited a week after he filled out and sent in the visitation form before he was approved for visits, then he headed straight there.

After showing his identification and signing in, he was granted access to the visitation room. The visitation room consisted of numerous chairs and tables, two water fountains, five vending machines, and a playroom for the kids with a TV and board games. Too-reel got two bottles of Coca-Cola and took a seat at a table, away from the guards' station. It had been more than ten years since they had seen each other face to face. He felt like a kid who was about to meet his long-lost father for the first time. As he thought about the last time he saw Jeff at his sentencing, he knew it was no coincidence that Jerol was now the same DA after him.

As he looked up, he saw a slim, tall man in a khaki uniform wearing a pair of white-on-white Air Force Ones approaching him. Too-reel did a double take. Yeah, that was Jeff. He had lost a few pounds, but he knew that Jamaican pimp walk with the limp anywhere he saw it. Jeff was six-feet-three-inches with curly hair and a full beard.

Too-reel stood with a huge smile on his face. The two men embraced while laughing.

"Boy, you got beef!" Jeff said in his Jamaican accent.

"I see you're losing a few pounds. What, they're not feeding you up here?"

"You know that I, mon, can't eat that bullshit they were feeding us. But since I've been here, I can cook my own shit with the microwave. Nothing but mackerel and dumplin's."

The two friends laughed as they sat down.

"So, what's going on?" Jeff asked.

"Nothing has changed. The fiends still smoke, the haters still hate, and the gold diggers are still digging. You ain't missing nothing."

"I spoke to mum yesterday. She said she had just received her monthly funds from you. She say you still good boy."

"What did you think, I was just going to cut you off?"

"Well, you know everyone else did. I guess they thought I was never going to see the light again. You know Sofia sent me divorce papers six months into my bid."

"Get the fuck out of here! Six months?"

Too-reel couldn't believe it. Sofia was Jeff's wife, and he had taken her in when she wasn't shit and gave her the world. Too-reel thought she would have given Jeff a few good years before she dipped.

Too-reel and Jeff talked for two hours, reminiscing about the past before Jeff finally got serious.

"I know that look in your eyes. What's really going on, Terell?"

"I'm in a little jam with Jerol."

"Jerol!" Jeff knew Jerol all too well. He was the one who had gotten him double life and was seeking the death penalty, which he didn't get. "What's the situation?"

"He's using my moms to make me work." Although Too-reel said it without any expression on his face, his eyes said it all. Jeff knew how hard this must be on him. Not only was his pride wounded, but his integrity was also damaged.

"How deep are you?"

"I'm committed."

Jeff leaned back in his seat. He took a deep breath.

"Terell, this is a very dirty game, and only a very small percentage make it out on top. Death is the only way out of this thing, whether it's by the cemetery or by the penitentiary. The other death is kind of what you're going through right now, the death I've been through."

"What do you mean?"

"Terell, when I first fell, to this day, you were the only one next to my mother who stood by me. We both knew the consequences of this game before we got involved and were ready to face them willingly, no matter what the outcome. Being locked down twenty-three hours a day gave me plenty of time to look back on my life. In that process, I've changed my way of thinking, my way of looking at things and seeing them for what they really are. My reality has changed. You were at my trial. You saw who came back to testify against me—almost everyone I took care of. The same guys who went to war with me and killed for me. In the end, all they cared about was themselves. It didn't matter what I did for them or how much. Shit, even Dei'z's son gave a statement against me."

"What? Does Dei'z know that?"

"Come on, mon. Him know everything else. Isn't Mannie still alive somewhere, living it up? That's exactly why I've decided I wasn't going to sit here and rot away, so I cut a deal with Jerol."

Too-reel was stunned.

"You what?"

"I gave up a couple of bodies and got my time cut to fifteen years. They're going to deport me back to Jamaica in five more years."

Too-reel couldn't believe what his mentor was telling him. He didn't want to believe it. This was the same guy who had molded him into who he was—his standards, his beliefs. This was a little too much for Too-reel. The visiting room started spinning. How could this be? Because of what Jeff's team had done to him, Too-reel hated all snitches with a passion and would kill them any chance he got. Jeff had now become one of the enemies.

"So you knew about what I was going through the whole time?" Too-reel looked at Jeff with contempt.

"I just found that out from you."

"Is that what this visit was about, to persuade me to join the team?"

"Come on, don't do this, Terell. You know the answer to that. This doesn't change me or how I feel about you."

"How do you figure that? You've become one of them. Of all the people, I would have never expected you."

"You know first-hand that we all have a weakness. And in the end, that weakness will cause you to do whatever they want you to do. You can't win by going against them, Terell. This is how it works, this is how it's been working. All the great players of the game have been doing it. Do you honestly think they've been ducking these guys for years? Everyone in the streets knows, so why don't they know? I'll tell you why. They do know. What's the number one code of the streets? Don't talk. But the streets are always talking. If you want to find something out, what do you do? Keep your ear to the streets. The elders only taught us these rules, and we accepted without consciously knowing so that they could use us as their scapegoats. The big fish gives up the little fish because they know they'll ride like you and me. Eventually, everyone's a possible snitch. If you love your kids, your wife, or even your mother, they'll find out and use that against you. Only the ones who ain't experienced this part of the game swear on what they won't do. But like me, the ones that have walked that road wish they had a chance to do it all over again. Don't wait till you get too far into the tunnel before it's too late."

Jeff looked at Too-reel's confused face.

"Fuck you! You're a Judas," Too-reel said as he got up and walked toward the exit.

"You know I'd never lie to you, Terell. All I can do is tell you the truth. This is how they play. Everybody only cares about themselves, you hear me? Don't let them fool you."

Too-reel kept walking until he was out of Jeff's sight.

As Too-reel was driving on the Jersey Turnpike, he thought

about his next move. But he was mostly thinking about what Jeff had said to him about Dei'z's son, Mannie. How could Dei'z act like that toward him if his own son was willing to testify against Jeff, who Dei'z knew was Too-reel's mentor?

A million thoughts raced through Too-reel's head—Vanessa and his baby, the idea of having a family. Then there was Deceive and where they were going with their relationship. Although she was his equal, and out of everyone else, he felt a strong connection with her, he wasn't in love with her, and he didn't know how he was going to explain the situation to Vanessa. He really hoped things would work out between them.

Too-reel was snapped out of his thoughts by the ringing of his phone. He grabbed it from his armrest and pressed send.

"Hello?"

"I'm not impressed. That fish was so small, I had to throw him back into the water. You're going to have to do much better than that if you want to keep your mother on the streets."

"I said I'll deliver, and that's what I'm going to do. I just need some more time."

"You have two days to deliver me another fish, and this one had better be a keeper. One more thing. The next time you decide you want to leave town without my consent, your mother will have to spend some time in our county jail." Jerol ended the call.

Too-reel's phone rang again before he got a chance to put it back down. He viewed the number before hitting send.

"Mickey, what's up?" he asked.

"Hey, buddy. How're you doing?"

"I'm just hanging in there."

"Well, that's good. I was just calling to give you an update about your boy, Pockets."

"What's up, Mick?"

"Well, the word on the streets is that he's working with the Feds. The guy did two controlled buys this week alone, and he's still on the streets, walking around. I don't know how long that's going to work before someone whacks that piece of shit. But in the meantime, I'll see what else I can dig up. I hope this guy wasn't foolish enough to bring up your name, but you know how it goes."

"Once again, I appreciate it, Mickey. I don't know what I'd do without you."

"For you, anytime."

At that moment, something Jeff had said kept playing over and over in his head. "If you have a weakness, they'll find it and use it against you—your kids, wife, or mother."

"One more thing I need you to do for me, Mickey."

"Whatever you need, kid."

"Jerol Highmon, he's the head DA for our district. I need you to find out about his background. His mother, if he has a wife, any kids, where he's from, things like that. And, oh yeah, I need to know where he lives. If you can work your magic, there'll be a huge payoff. And I'm going to need photos, too."

"That's a pretty big order, also dangerous, but since it's you, I'll get on it right away."

"That's why I love you."

Once Too-reel hung up with Mickey, he started thinking about how he was going to buy some extra time with Jerol.

Chapter 12

Burgull and Maloy were pulling out of Dunkin' Donuts when Burgull received a call.

"Yeah, Burgull."

"It's Valdimire."

"What do you want?"

"Remember the picture of that girl you showed me the other day?"

"Yeah," Burgull replied with more interest.

"I have two customers in here right now, and one of them looks like her."

"I'm ten minutes away. Try to keep them there. I don't care if you give something away, just do it! I'm sending a squad car there right now."

"You owe me a favor—" Valdimire didn't get a chance to finish the sentence before Burgull hung up.

"Diamond District. Now! And send a squad car over to Girl's Best Friend."

Burgull grabbed the switch that turned on the sirens as Maloy floored the gas pedal.

Babydoll was with a target she had just met two days earlier. At least that was what she had told Cruddy. She had been exchanging one of the outfits that Cocaine had gotten her from the Gucci store when she met him. Although she wasn't supposed to be mixing business with pleasure, she found Dennis attractive and decided to let him take her out, although she didn't think he had the kind of money Cruddy was looking for. She was supposed to be out on a job, but since Cruddy was so caught up in the Tito situation and moving, she figured she would be overlooked.

Dennis was picking up two rings for his boss. He worked for a real estate company, but the whole time, he acted like the rings were for him. He was trying to impress Babydoll after he saw how high maintenance she looked. He was about to tell her he was just getting started in the real estate business and wasn't as rich as he had claimed to be, but when he saw the diamond necklace she wore, he changed his mind.

"Whoo, look at that ring over there. It's just to die for," Babydoll said as she pointed at the thirteen-carat yellow diamond ring.

"You like that, ma'am? That's an excellent choice. She does have great taste in jewelry, wouldn't you say so, sir?" Valdimire commented as he served the couple from behind the glass counter.

"Yes, she does," Dennis replied.

"It's on sale for thirty thousand. Quite a steal, if I say so myself. Would the missus like to try it on?"

"Oh, we're not mar—"

"Why, yes, I would." Babydoll cut Dennis off before he could finish his sentence. Valdimire used a key from around his neck to open the glass door and retrieved the ring.

"Here you go, ma'am." Babydoll stuck out her hand and allowed Valdimire to slide the ring onto her finger. "Perfect fit."

Babydoll held up her hand in front of the mirror on top of the counter as she checked out the glistening ring. "Baby, what do you think?" she asked Dennis as she held the ring in front of his face.

"It's, uh, beautiful," Dennis replied in a nervous voice.

"Would you like me to put it on your company's tab, along with the other two rings, sir?"

"No, no, wait a minute. Now isn't the right time."

"You'll receive a twenty-percent discount since this would be your third purchase in one day."

Valdimire kept Dennis and Babydoll in the store until he spotted Burgull with two agents and four officers. Burgull immediately recognized Babydoll from the tape.

"Excuse me, miss, I have some questions I would like to ask you," Burgull said as he approached Babydoll. The other officers surrounded the couple.

"Wha-what's going on, Trisha?" Dennis asked.

"That's what I would like to know!" Babydoll yelled.

"Why don't you explain to this nice gentleman how you seduce innocent guys like him for a living before you rob them blind and leave them tied naked to their beds?"

Babydoll's eyes got big as she tried to make a dash.

"Sorry, honey. Not today. You won't get away that easy."

Burgull grabbed Babydoll by her collar, popped the necklace, and examined it before looking back at Babydoll. It was the same necklace she had robbed from his son.

"Oh, shit! What's Babydoll doing down here?" Egypt asked as she and Bangout watched Burgull bring her outside in cuffs and place her in the backseat of their truck.

"Cruddy's not going to like this," Bangout replied.

"Listen, Cocaine said she'll be sitting in the car while this dude makes the drop. They're supposed to be here by one, which is in a few minutes."

Cruddy glanced at his watch.

"I don't want no one to make a move until he walks up to the van."

"What kind of car is he driving, and what color is the money van?" Cutter asked as he slipped on his black leather gloves.

"The kid Cocaine's fucking with is supposed to be in a black CL500 Benz coupe. The Caravan is sky blue, I think."

"Well, it looks like Cocaine's boy is about to pull up," D-Range replied from the back seat.

D-Range was usually a shadow for one of the girls, but Cruddy was using him because he was cool under pressure and would shoot first and ask questions later.

The black coupe pulled up right across from where Cruddy was parked, unaware of them. The tints on the Benz's window were too dark for Cruddy to see inside the car.

"Get down," he told his boys as they all slumped in their seats. Their car windows were also tinted. Cutter had two black 9 mms resting in his lap while D-Range toted a baby AR handgun. Cruddy had two blue steel snub-nose .38s. They sat patiently for ten minutes before the Caravan rounded the corner.

"Heads up, fellas. This might be it." The Caravan slowed down as it approached the Benz before pulling in front of it and stopping. The Benz's door opened as a slim, tall, light-skinned kid stepped out with a shopping bag in his hand.

"That's him. I see Cocaine in the passenger seat. This kid is supposed to be dangerous. If he makes any moves, air him out," Cruddy said. The driver of the Benz walked around the hood of his car and went to the passenger side of the Caravan.

"Go! Go! Go!" Cruddy yelled as he popped his door and jumped out with guns in hand. Cutter was right behind him as they ran across the street, heading toward the passenger side of the Caravan. D-Range ran toward the driver's side of the van.

Blue was saying something to the light-skinned kid when he saw two figures run across the street, and one run behind the van.

"Look out!" he yelled.

By the time Rock looked behind him and started to reach for his gun, it was too late.

Bup! Bup! Bup! Bup!

The first two shots hit him in his chest while another went in his stomach. The other bullet entered his thigh. The impact spun him around, throwing him into the car that was parked next to the van before he fell to the ground.

"Pull off! Pull off!" Hype shouted as he slammed the door shut.

Bup! Bup! Bup! Bup!

A few more shots flew through the side of the Caravan's door. One hit Hype in the shoulder, sending him flying to the middle row of seats. Before Blue could shift the van into drive, a gun barrel came straight through his window, sending shattered glass everywhere.

"Get the fuck out before I splatter you all over this bitch!" D-Range yelled.

D-Range opened the door and grabbed Blue out of his seat. Blue got tangled up in his seat belt, so D-Range hit him in his forehead with the butt of the gun, thinking he was holding on to something before realizing he was snagged.

"Unbuckle that shit!" Blue did as he was told as blood trickled down his face. As soon as the seatbelt snapped, Blue was dragged out and thrown to the street.

"Lay the fuck down!" D-Range yelled as he waved the gun in Blue's face. Cruddy and Cutter were already in back of the Caravan. They grabbed Hype's bloody body and tossed him out of the van and onto the pavement. Cruddy jumped into the driver's seat and threw the van into drive as Cutter slammed the side door shut. The Caravan took off.

D-Range ran back to the car they had arrived in and pulled out behind the van. Cocaine hopped in the driver's seat of the Benz and pulled out behind D-Range. Blue had to roll out of the way or get run over by the Benz. He watched as they pulled off down the block before he got up and ran over to Hype.

"Yo, Hype. You a'ight?"

There was no response.

"Hype! Hype! Hype!" He kept shaking Hype's body.

"Come on, nigga, get up! Get up!" He kept shouting as he shook Hype's lifeless body. People started to crowd the street as the sounds of sirens were heard in the distance.

"How are we doing today, Agent Tyson?" Jerol asked as Vanessa walked inside his office.

"I'm fine, sir."

"Please have a seat and close the door."

"I don't mean to be rude, but I didn't come here for any small talk. Let's just get straight to the point because I'm just getting back in good with Too-reel."

"I'm glad to see you're on top of your job, but please take a seat. This won't take long. Besides, you look a little flushed. Are you OK?"

"Yes, I'm fine." Vanessa closed the door behind her. She didn't bother to sit down.

"You also seem to have gained a few pounds since we last saw each other. Living good, are we?"

"I know you didn't call me all the way down here to tell me how fat I've gotten, sir."

"You're right, Agent Tyson, I didn't. Now, I know you are deep into this case, not only on a physical level but also on an emotional level."

Jerol paused for a moment.

"Before you even consider having this baby, I want you to realize what kind of person you're dealing with. Mr. Cobe cannot be trusted, and you should know the truth."

Jerol opened his desk drawer and pulled out a yellow envelope. He handed it to Vanessa and pretended not to see the surprised look on her face. He knew she didn't think they knew she was pregnant, or that she had plans of keeping it.

"What is this?" Vanessa asked as she opened the envelope.

She was instantly hurt by what she saw. As bad as she wanted to cry, she held herself together. She wasn't going to let Jerol see her break down. She showed no emotion as she handed the envelope back to Jerol.

"Why are you showing me this?"

"Like I said, you're deep into the case, and I don't want you to forget which side you're playing for. He's only using you, my dear."

"It's no different from what you're doing. I know what team I'm playing for. I'm only doing what was asked of me by you. What you should be asking yourself is what kind of games you're playing with people's lives. If that's all you called me down here to show me, then I'm ready to leave, if that's all right with you." Vanessa stared at Jerol with anger in her eyes. She knew the game he was playing.

"I didn't mean to upset you, Agent Tyson. I wouldn't want to be the cause of you losing that baby you're carrying. So, yes, you may leave."

Vanessa stormed out of Jerol's office, not even bothering to close the door. Jerol smiled as he glanced at the photographs in the envelope of Too-reel and Deceive having sex while they were in Mexico.

Vanessa hurried out of the building, hoping she wouldn't encounter anyone she knew. As she hit the parking garage, the tears poured down her cheeks.

How could he do this to me? He said nothing was going on between them. How long has this been going on? Why is Terell doing this to me? Why? Vanessa wondered as she approached her car.

As she pulled out of the garage, she pulled straight into traffic, cutting off two oncoming cars and almost causing a serious accident. Vanessa found herself driving around with no direction. She needed to talk to someone.

Without consciously knowing where she was going, she ended up parked right in front of Ms. Cobe's house. Vanessa was parked there ten minutes with her engine running before someone tapped on her window. When she looked over to her passenger side, she saw Ms. Cobe. She forced a smile to her face as she rolled down the window.

"Hello, Ms. Cobe."

"What's the matter, Vanessa? Why don't you come on inside so we can talk."

"I really don't want to bother you with my problems."

"Nonsense. Turn off the car and come on in."

Ms. Cobe turned and walked back to the house. Vanessa turned off the car and checked herself in the rearview mirror. Her makeup was a little smeared and runny from crying. She retrieved some wet wipes from the glove compartment and cleaned her face before exiting the car. The front door was left open for her. She entered and closed the door behind her.

"Take a seat in the living room. I'll be there in a minute," Ms. Cobe shouted from the kitchen. Vanessa did as she was told and walked into the living room. She took a seat on the largest of three couches. She glanced at the fifty-two-inch flat screen that hung on the wall. *Days of our Lives* was on. Right above the TV was a framed photo of Ms. Cobe in her younger days, alongside Too-reel. He looked to be no more than five years old. Even though she was mad at him, Vanessa couldn't help but crack a smile at how adorable he looked, even with a mean-mug expression. That picture made her smile every time she saw it.

"Even as a little boy, we couldn't get him to smile. He was such a serious little boy, and never liked to play too many games," Ms. Cobe said as she entered the living room carrying a tray with two slices of cake and two cups of tea. Another small dish contained slices of lemon while a bowl held sugar in it. Ms. Cobe took a seat next to Vanessa as she placed the tray down on top of the marble and glass coffee table. She then handed Vanessa a cup with tea and a small spoon.

"You may want to sweeten yours a little. Too much sugar isn't good for me. Besides, I had a piece of cake already."

"Thank you." Vanessa added a few teaspoons of sugar to her tea and stirred. After a few minutes of silence, Ms. Cobe spoke.

"I know the look of love and regrets all too well, my dear. As of late, I've noticed those two things in your eyes. Life is a blessing, and to live life means to make mistakes. When you make mistakes, only two things can come out of it: either you learn from them, or you continue to repeat them. Life is what you make it. Some things you can change. Others, you have to live with. In the end, it all boils down to what's best for you."

"I have something I want to tell you, and I hope it won't make you look at me any differently. My name is not Vanessa. It's Christal Tyson, and I'm a federal agent. I was sent undercover to get close to Terell so the government could take him down. I swear in the beginning, I was only doing my job, but in the process of doing my job, I fell in love with Terell."

Tears began to roll down Vanessa's face. She started sniffling as she continued to talk.

"I-I tried to get them to pull me out, but they wouldn't."

Sniff, sniff.

"Now they're using you to make Terell cooperate with them, or they're going to arrest you. It's all my fault!"

Vanessa held her head down. She couldn't bear to look in Ms. Cobe's face.

"I've . . . I've tried to prove to him that I . . . I love him by betraying my job, but I don't think he will ever forgive me. I'm pregnant with his baby, and I don't know if I should keep it. I don't want my child growing up and not knowing his father."

"There, there, child. You're being too hard on yourself." Ms. Cobe embraced Vanessa and rubbed her back.

"But he hates me. What can I do? I saw him with another woman!" Ms. Cobe grabbed Vanessa by her shoulders and eased her up so she could look in her face.

"He doesn't hate you. Let me tell you something. That boy has never once in his thirty years of life brought anyone home to meet me. You are the only person or female he has ever let set foot in this house, and that says a lot to me. Now Terell has always been a very bitter young man—very controlling and revengeful because of his father not choosing to be a part of his life. He would always ask me as a boy why his father didn't love him, and I really didn't have an answer. For that reason alone, I know if you do choose to have that baby, he will not turn his back on you or that child. As far as you gaining his trust back, time heals all wounds. I'm not saying it will be easy, but if you two truly love one another, you will find a way. That also includes the situation you two are facing with your job. As for me, the Lord will protect me, and if I know my son, he's not going to allow anyone to keep the upper hand on him."

"I really want to make this work."

"You can, my dear. You can."

Chapter 13

It didn't take Cruddy and his crew long to open the stash box hidden in the van's floor. Cruddy took the van to a local mechanic shop off Liberty Avenue in Queens, where he had a friend hook up a device to the fuse box. The device caused all the electronically operated devices on the van to go on and off or open and close.

Once they got the stash open, they cleaned it out. Cruddy paid his man for the job and left him the Benz Cocaine drove, the van, and their getaway vehicle. Since the shop was an undercover chop shop, leaving the vehicles was a bonus for the mechanic. But what seemed to the mechanic as Cruddy looking out for him was actually insurance to tie the chop shop owner to the robbery. Cruddy wanted to make sure the owner would also have something to lose for talking. Now his hands were just as dirty as Cruddy's and his crew's.

Cruddy had his silver Expedition with tinted, smoke-gray windows at the shop so they could switch vehicles. Cocaine took the driver's seat while Cruddy and Cutter sat in the back with D-Range in the passenger seat. As they were heading back to Cruddy's spot, he noticed his cell phone kept beeping, indicating he had a voicemail. He retrieved it and checked his missed calls. All three calls were from Bangout and Egypt. He hit his scroll until he came to Bangout's number. He pressed send and waited.

"What's up? What? When did this happen? A'ight, I'm on my way to the spot. I'll see if I can get D to find out what's going on with her." Cruddy ended the call.

"Shit!"

"What's wrong?" Cocaine asked with alarm.

"They got Babydoll."

"Who got her?" Cutter asked.

"The Feds. They picked her up downtown in the district."

"What was she doing there?" Cocaine was really thinking out loud and hadn't meant to voice her opinion.

"That's what I'd like to know," Cruddy said.

"Oh, shit, Daddy. Look!" As soon as Cocaine turned onto the block where Cruddy lived, they saw federal agents setting up. They looked like they were just about to burst into Cruddy's house. "What should I do, Daddy?"

"Just keep driving. Don't stop."

Cruddy and Cutter clutched their guns as they slid down into their seats in the back. Cocaine did as she was told and kept driving past the house.

"That's that fucking guy in the picture. The director. How the fuck did he know I was staying here?" Everyone in the car thought the same thing.

"How long ago did they say Baby got picked up?" Cutter asked.

"A few hours ago," Cruddy replied through clenched teeth. Cruddy's phone started ringing. He screened it before answering.

"Yo!" Cruddy replied but didn't get an answer. "Yo?" he yelled into the phone again. All he could make out was a lot of scuffling in the background.

"Put your hands behind your back!" he heard someone say over the phone.

"I got the girl," someone else said.

"Hello? Who's on this line? This is the FBI. Who is this?" someone said into the phone.

Cruddy clicked off his phone. Cutter saw the look on his face and knew something was wrong.

"What is it?" Cutter asked.

"They got Egypt and Bangout."

The car got quiet again.

"What are we going to do?" Cocaine asked, becoming a little panicked.

"Just drive. Let me figure things out for a minute. We need to get off the road. Head toward Jersey. D-Range, call Wolf and fill him in. Tell him to be careful and round up the rest of the gang and wait for my next call. And tell him not to go to any of the spots Babydoll knows about."

Hype and Rock were rushed to Jamaica Hospital in Queens. Blue was treated for minor injuries while Hype was listed in stable condition. The bullet had passed clean through his shoulder. Rock, on the other hand, was listed in critical condition. He was rushed into emergency surgery.

Blue managed to sneak out of the hospital and call Too-reel. He filled him in on what had taken place. They both knew it would be only a matter of time before the detectives came asking questions.

Instead of waiting for Too-reel to pick them up, Blue wheeled Hype's weak body out in a wheelchair and hailed a cab. He then used all his strength to put Hype in the back of the cab, leaving the wheelchair on the side of the street. He called Too-reel back from a payphone and had him meet them in Brooklyn. Too-reel took Hype to a friend's house who was a nurse at Brooklyn Hospital. She usually took care of any wounds for Too-reel and his crew that didn't need emergency room attention. Hype's shoulder was cleaned and dressed, then put into a sling.

Word quickly got around on the streets about what had happened, and Too-reel's phone was blowing up. The streets were like that. Somehow, some way, someone always knew or saw what happened.

Deceive and Ice were two of the only people Too-reel spoke with. He kept it brief and told them where he was. Within an hour, Deceive and Ice were at the nurse's house, sitting in the living room.

"Refreshments are in the fridge. When you're finished here, just lock up when you leave," the nurse said.

"Thank you, Jackie. I'll talk to you later," Too-reel replied.

"And you, baby, put some food in that body of yours," she told Hype. "Don't forget to have someone change the pad on your wound tonight before you go to sleep. Those painkillers I gave you should ease the pain a whole lot."

"Thank you for your help, ma'am," Hype replied in a weak voice. Jackie exited the house, closing the door behind her.

"Who did this to y'all?" Ice asked as he hopped out of his seat the minute the door closed. He began to pace. He was ready for blood now.

"Take it easy, Ice," Too-reel said.

"Like I was saying, they must have been waiting for us. By the time I noticed them, it was too late," Hype said.

"What did they look like?" Ice asked.

"I didn't see shit. I just heard Blue say, 'Look out,' then I saw

Rock get hit up. I tried to close the door, then all I remembered after that was feeling something hot," Hype said as he touched his shoulder and frowned from the soreness.

"The only person I saw was the guy who dragged me out of the van," Blue said.

"What did he look like?" Ice asked again, getting angrier and angrier the more he heard.

"Calm down, Ice, and let them finish telling us what happened. We're all upset about this."

"These niggas think shit's sweet. I'm going to make someone pay for this shit!" Ice said.

"Who's going to pay? Believe me, I want them just as bad as you do, but we've got to get to the bottom of this thing before we can even make a move. Rock always picked a new spot every week, so the question is, how did they know where y'all was going to meet him. Someone else must have known," Too-reel said as he tried to piece the puzzle together.

"Rock had someone else in the car with him. After they threw me and Hype out of the van and pulled off, Rock's Benz pulled off behind them."

"Did y'all get a look at who it was? I mean, a male or a female?" Deceive asked.

"I bet you it had to be one of them bitches he be fucking with!" Ice said. "That motherfucker might be a gangster in the streets, but he's a sucker for a pretty face. And when he gets drunk, he be running his fucking mouth too much. I'll put my life on it that this is his fault. He better not pull through or I'm going to finish the job on his stupid ass."

"Ice, check this out. I'm going to need you to be cool until I do some more homework. I'm going to check with Rock's people at the spot and find out who he was with last when he left to make the drop-off. Hopefully, they'll be able to shed some light on the situation. In the meantime, the money we already collected is going to be moved to another location. The drop is supposed to be in the next two days, but I'm going to make it tomorrow night. I want you and Hitman to stay on top of this thing. Let me find out who was with Rock while you follow any other leads. Hype, I want you to go home and rest."

"Man, I'm good. I can handle this."

"Blue, make sure you take him home, and he's straight before you leave him. I want to run down something to you a little later. I'll call when I'm ready. Deceive, I'm going to need your half of that paper by the morning."

"No problem."

"I'm going to go holla at Rock's people. Deceive, could you drop off Hype and Blue? Ice, go shake a few trees and see what falls out, but take it easy. We don't want to scare no one off."

"I got this. This is what I get paid for."

"Whoever took the van must have had a spot nearby to take it to," Too-reel said. "Maybe a warehouse, a mechanic's shop, or a junkyard. More than likely a chop shop. Get some of your people to check around for some parts, Ice."

"What? Van parts?" Ice asked.

"No. Benz parts. They might get rid of the van, but the Benz is worth money. If you can find the Benz, we can find the robbers. Zone out the area and start from a ten-mile radius. Find out who runs a chop shop in those areas. Break some arms or grease some palms. If anyone knows anything, it's going to be the fiends."

"And you said to take it easy."

"Well, you know what I mean, cowboy."

*****

"Baby!" Egypt yelled as an agent brought her into the room where they were holding Babydoll in a small cell. The agent told Babydoll to stand up and face the wall as he opened the cell door and placed Egypt inside. After closing it, he opened the tray slot and told Egypt to place her wrists through it so he could unlock the cuffs. Once her cuffs were off, and the agents left the room, the two hugged and began to talk.

"What the fuck are you doing here, Egypt?"

"Shit, I don't know. They just snatched me and Bangout when we stopped by his house. We didn't even get a chance to get out of the car."

"They got Bangout's prints off some receipt. I heard that asshole agent when his government name came back. Plus, whatever name Cruddy was using was on the account that Tito had. Apparently, he was using the same name on one of his houses."

"Oh, shit. Which one?" Egypt asked, her eyes wide open.

"I don't know. I just hope they don't get him."

"Baby, what the fuck were you doing in that jewelry store?"

Baby's mouth dropped.

"How did you know they caught me in the jewelry store?"

"We were following that fat motherfucker that got you. You forgot."

"Does Cruddy know?"

"Yep! What were you doing anyway?"

"I was just chilling with this guy I kind of like. He was picking up something from that store."

"How did they know you were there, and why did they arrest you?"

"I don't know how they knew I was there. That white guy I got the night of that big party, his father, who's a cop, happens to be the asshole that got me."

"Oh, shit."

"Yeah, and he's even got a tape with me and his son in the house that night. He also got a picture of Wolf. He kept asking me who he was."

"That still doesn't explain why they got me and Bangout."

"I think it's from that day they went to pick up some money from Tito."

"Oh, yeah. They did say they were being followed. That still don't mean shit. Why am I here? You, on the other hand, yeah, but they don't really have nothing on me or Bangout for that matter."

Even though the girls were whispering, everything they said was being recorded. The cell was bugged and had been set up for this purpose. The girls were being monitored from a secret room.

"She's right, I don't have anything on her and this Bangout character," Burgull said. I want you to run the other two names through the system and see what we come up with. Anyone with the name Cruddy or Wolf, I want to see their files."

"What about the two we picked up today? Aren't we going to do something with them?" Agent Newkirk asked.

"Hold them for the next three days, then let them go."

"What? Just like that? Scot-free? There must be a law against following a government agent. You can't just let them go like that. Aren't you curious about why they were following you?"

"Can't you see, agent, these are not your average street thugs. If they wouldn't have picked the wrong kid to rob, who knows if we would have ever stumbled upon them. There is a brain at the head of this operation, and I intend to find out who this Cruddy guy is. Like the girl said, we don't have anything on them yet, so when we release them, hopefully, they will lead us to this guy, and we can take down this ring of robbers.

"In the meantime, run all of their prints with any unsolved house invasions where the victims were left gagged and bound. Most of these victims will more than likely be males who claimed to be kidnapped or ambushed. In the end, the leader's smarts might backfire on him. Even though this isn't a federal case, I'm pretty sure the DA will come to an agreement with me. I also want you to put the word out on these two guys. Let's see if any of our informants know their names. Someone is always looking to help himself."

"What the hell is going on, Deceive?" Sonia asked as she dropped off the shopping bag with vacuum-sealed money inside.

"Too-reel is changing the drop to tomorrow."

"But the drop isn't for another two days. Plus, that's not all the money."

Sonia walked over to Deceive and knelt down, holding down one side of the vacuum sealer as Deceive clamped down on the other and hit the start button.

Vuuuuuu!

The vacuum sealer sucked all the air from the shopping bag and sealed it shut. Once the process was completed, the red light changed to green, signaling it was successful.

"What time tomorrow are they going to be ready?" Sonia asked as she and Deceive began to stuff another bag with money.

"He just said tomorrow. More than likely it will be in the morning."

"Same place?"

"The pickup is now the drop-off. He changed up on everything."

"After what happened to Hype and Blue, who will be driving the money in the morning?"

"I don't know, but I'm pretty sure he'll have Ice and someone following the van."

"How's Hype, by the way?"

"He's a'ight. The bullet didn't hit anything major. It was a clean shot."

"Did you see the wound?"

"It was dressed by the time I got there. But it's a pretty big hole in his shoulder."

"Damn. So Man is running around with Ice now?"

"Yeah, they're trying to find out who did this."

"That's not a good combination." Sonia raised her eyebrow.

"Tell me about it," Deceive said, totally agreeing.

Early the next morning, a dark brown van pulled out of the garage of Caribbean Shipping, a small-barrel shipping company off Clarkson Avenue in the East Flatbush area of Brooklyn. The van made a right turn onto Clarkson, headed toward Utica Avenue. The light on the corner of Fifty-first Street turned red as the van approached. As the driver of the van stopped and waited, he reached into his top pocket and retrieved a pack of Newports and a yellow Bic lighter. He turned the pack upside down and tapped out a cigarette. He placed the cigarette in his mouth, then placed the pack back into his top pocket.

As he lit the cigarette and took two deep drags, a black SUV pulled up right in front of him from the opposite side of the street. Two navy-blue Impalas pulled up to his side while two other SUVs pulled up behind him.

What the fuck is going on? the driver wondered as agents jumped from their vehicles, all pointing their guns in his direction.

"Put your hands in the air!"

"Turn off your vehicle!" another agent yelled. The driver was so scared, the cigarette fell from his mouth as he held up his hands. Another agent snatched open his door and threw him to the ground.

"What the hell is going on?" the driver yelled in a strong Trinidadian accent. Meanwhile, Brody was leading another group of agents inside the shipping company.

Too-reel was at one of his stash houses. No one knew about this house, not even his mother. This was where he kept all his cash. He had two built-in safes behind the wall of one of his apartments. He had purchased the building from the city for a dollar and fixed it up. The building was in an alias name and was being rented out by an agency. The money he collected for rent went to an account that was then transferred to another account he had set up offshore. He never touched that money. It just collected interest.

Too-reel had just finished boxing up all the money for the drop.

He was up all night, double checking the count. His cell phone went off.

"Yo!"

"There's a leak in your organization. They just busted a van with your money," the voice on the other end stated.

"What money?"

"We got a tip from a female that you had a van dropping off money to a secret location." Too-reel's heart jumped out of his chest. Deceive was the only person he had told about the drop-off. Could Vanessa have been right?

"That drop-off was canceled, but thanks for the heads up."

The line went dead as Too-reel put his phone down. The only reason he hadn't made the drop was because the money was short, and he had to check it again. It was very unusual for the money Deceive gave him to be short. In all the years of them doing business, the money had never come up short. Too-reel didn't want to believe Deceive had something to do with the raid, but the one thing the game was teaching him was that he couldn't trust anyone.

As he sat deep in thought, he came up with a plan to flush out the snitch in his crew.

Chapter 14

"This is where he said he saw them pull in," Hitman's cousin said as they pulled across the street from a mechanic's shop connected to a small junkyard off Liberty Avenue.

"You sure that crackhead knows what the fuck he's talking about? Because if this is a runaround for a quick blast, I'm going to put sparks up his ass for real," Ice said as he looked back at Hitman's cousin.

"Nah, don't nothing go down in this hood without Dusty knowing about it. If a nigga fart, Dusty can tell you who did it and what they ate."

"How do you plan on handling this?" Man asked as she pulled up beside Ice's car.

"The way I always handle things." Ice held up his gun in the air for Man to see as he cocked it.

"Nah, let me try something first. If it doesn't work, we'll do it your way."

Man parked her truck and got out. She tucked her shirt into her pants and pulled her pants above her waist. Now her baggy pants hugged her ass and thighs. She took off her NY fitted cap and threw it in the back seat of her truck before crossing the street to the mechanic's shop.

"Damn, I didn't know she had an ass that fat," Hitman's cousin said.

"Neither did I," Ice said as he and Hitman both watched her strut inside the shop, switching her ass like a model strutting down the runway.

Zipppp! Bang! Bang! Bang! Zooo! was all Man heard when she walked into the work area of the garage. Cars were jacked up with guys standing underneath them, while other cars had just the hoods open and were being checked out with all types of wires and cables running from them. An elderly man in a faded blue jumpsuit with oil stains all over him approached her.

"What can I do for you, pretty lady?" he asked.

"I was looking for the owner," Man replied in a sweet voice.

"He's in the back office." The old man pointed toward the back, in the direction of the office. Man watched her step as she tiptoed over tools and puddles of grease and oil. Every guy she passed looked up to get a view of her ass.

When she made it to the back, a chubby, dark-skinned man was on the phone. When he looked up and saw Man, he held up his index finger. After he finished his conversation, he hung up the phone and gave Man his full attention.

"Yes, what can I do for you?"

"I feel kind of awkward doing this, but a cousin of mine told me about this place." Man placed her finger in her mouth as if she was nervous and crossed her legs.

"What did he tell you?"

"I kind of had an accident the other day. I crashed my car. I didn't report it to my insurance because it would send my premiums sky high, so I was hoping to fix it myself. It will be cheaper in the long run."

"Where is this cousin of yours from?"

"He's from Ozone, off the Van Wyck."

"And where are you from?"

"North Hampton, Long Island."

The man looked Man up and down. He could tell by her clothes she wasn't an average girl from the hood. Even though she wasn't dressed up, he could smell money on her. *Little rich girl all the way in the hood*, he thought as he licked his lips.

"What kind of car do you drive?"

"A Mercedes."

"What kind?"

"SL500."

"What part are you looking for?"

"A passenger side door and front headlight. Can you help me?" Man batted her eyes.

"Yeah, but it's not going to be cheap. That's a Mercedes."

"Well, money ain't the problem."

Just what he wanted to hear.

"Follow me."

The owner led Man to the junkyard where all the scrap parts were kept, along with numerous crashed and junked cars. He walked Man to a small shack with a lock on the door. He took out a key and unlocked the door, then they entered the shack. He hit a switch on the wall, turning on the light. There were shelves with all types of parts on them. Car doors hung from the ceiling, along with fenders and lights. The room was clean and cool. The owner walked up to a sanded-down door that was on one shelf.

"This should fit. What year is your car?"

"Oh-eight," Man replied as she inspected the door. She could tell the door was once black from a few patches of colored spots. When she looked at the mirror on the door, she saw the initial imprint of the letter R. Rock had an R initial on all his vehicles. That was when she knew for sure this door had come from Rock's car.

"You're lucky because this door is pretty new," the owner said.

"How much will the door and headlights cost?"

"The door alone is going to run you two grand. I'll take five for the headlights." Man knew he was trying to take advantage of her because she was a woman.

"So, that's twenty-five hundred."

"That's right."

"Can you bring the parts up front while I go grab the money from my car. Is cash OK?"

"I wouldn't prefer it any other way."

"Thank you. You're a lifesaver." Man walked off, switching her ass as the owner stood and watched with a smile on his face. Not because of the view, but because of the money he was about to receive.

Man walked back to her truck and grabbed both of her guns before letting Ice know this was the spot. All three men exited the car and followed Man back to the mechanic's shop. Ice and Hitman pulled down the shutter to the garage when they walked inside. Man and Hitman's cousin turned the open sign on the front door to closed as they locked the door behind them.

"Good work, cousin. I'll be in contact." Cruddy had just finished talking to D. "No wonder this cracker's persistent. That white boy Baby took turns out to be his son. Because of that bitch and this cracker, I've lost most of my money!"

Cruddy had over a half million in cash at the house the Feds raided, which D told Cruddy they had recovered. The only good thing was that they had just hit Too-reel's stash van for a little over six hundred thousand dollars. This one little incident with Baby had destroyed his whole operation overnight.

"We need to get the fuck out of dodge," Cutter stated.

"Not before I pay this motherfucker back for fucking up my hustle."

"How do you plan on doing that?"

"I'm going to find out where he lives and personally watch him take his last breath. Then we'll leave."

Cutter didn't like the sound of that. He knew killing a federal agent, especially a director, would give them global press, which he didn't want to have any part of. Cutter wasn't ready to go back to prison for the rest of his natural life yet. *This might be a problem*, he thought.

After being held for three days, Bangout and Egypt were released, and Bangout was given his truck back. While they were driving, neither one spoke a word. Both suspected the truck had been bugged. Bangout also noticed they were being followed.

"I'm hungry as fuck. Pull over and let me get some food," Egypt said.

Bangout pulled over next to a Chinese restaurant. They got out and walked inside the restaurant.

"You know we're being followed, right?" Bangout asked.

"Yeah, I saw the gray Impala."

"I'm going to use a pay phone and let them know we're good."

"Tell them Babydoll didn't say anything and she's holding it down to the fullest. Tell Cruddy they got her for that shit with the white boy and I don't know if they'll give her bond. You know how the Feds work."

"Got it."

Bangout walked outside as Egypt placed her order. He spotted the gray Impala as he walked down the street to a payphone. He didn't want to call Cruddy's phone, so he called Cocaine's cell instead and hoped the bootlegged number was still working. Bootleg phones sometimes lasted only a day, but sometimes lasted up to a year.

"Hello," Cocaine answered.

"Ocaine Ca." Bangout started talking in gibberish code, something they had all practiced for situations like this. The key to gibberish was taking the first letter of a word and placing it at the end of the word with the letter A. So 'yes' would be 'esya'.

"Angba," Cocaine replied. Conversation continued in gibberish.

"Yeah, let me holla at Cruddy." After a few seconds of silence, Cruddy got on the phone.

"Yo!"

"We're being followed. But otherwise, we're good."

"Do you. If anything, I'll find y'all."

"What about Babydoll? She's holding it down."

"Fuck Baby! Her stupid ass is the reason they're on to us in the first place."

"But she didn't say shit."

"You heard what the fuck I said. Cutter was right. She's been fucking up. She brought this on herself."

Bangout didn't like what Cruddy was doing to Babydoll, but he couldn't do anything about it. Cruddy was their boss, and Cutter was his buddy, but the fact that he would just leave one of his soldiers behind wounded, with no help, turned Bangout off. Yeah, Babydoll might have to do some time, but the least he could have done was get her a lawyer and fill her account with some money. Bangout knew how it felt to be in prison with no outside help. He told himself he was going to bless Babydoll's account the first chance he got.

"A'ight, one," Bangout said.

Cruddy clicked off without replying. Bangout walked back to the restaurant and told Egypt what Cruddy had said.

"So he's just going to leave her like that?" Egypt was surprised.

"That's what he said. He said we should just do us."

"What does that mean?"

"You figure it out. He's your everything." Egypt didn't want to believe what Bangout was saying. There was no way Cruddy would just leave her and Babydoll, or any of them for that matter. He loved them, at least that was what she thought.

As Jerol shuffled around some paperwork, his private line beeped. He pressed the speaker button, answering the phone at the same time.

"Yeah? To where?"

"One-two-three-six Nostrand Avenue, a Golden Krust bakery,

around seven tonight."

"That's only an hour from now. I hope you're right this time."

Jerol ended the call.

Too-reel sat patiently awaiting the call that was sure to come. He had changed the location of the pickup and had purposely given Deceive, Sonia, Tabisha, and Man all different locations at the very last minute. He figured whoever's route got raided, she would be the leak. As much as he wanted to fill Deceive in on what was going on, he had doubts about trusting her. This whole ordeal had put him in a paranoid state of mind. What Jeff had said finally started making sense to him. Jeff wasn't telling him he should cooperate or become a snitch. He was just letting him know exactly what he was going up against, and that he shouldn't trust anyone. The same guys who killed for you would kill you. The same guys who were willing to die for you, wouldn't do a day in prison for you.

Too-reel had a flashback of Jeff schooling him on the art of war when he was much younger.

Jeff said, "Remember, you may be able to beat someone physically, but they can always heal and come back to be twice as strong. The best way to defeat someone is from the inside out."

"How do you do that?" Too-reel asked.

"Mentally. This way they will develop a phobia of you. Just the mere thought of your presence will scare them. Don't just kill their body. Destroy their soul, their mind. We live inside our minds. Always remember that your best friend could be your worst enemy."

Too-reel was snapped back to reality by the ringing of his phone.

"Yo!"

"They bit," a voice replied on the other line.

"What route?"

"That bitch Sonia!" Ice replied.

"Round up everyone and meet me at the spot at ten. Deceive and the rest of the girls will be there, too."

"I'm going to punish that bitch!"

"No, that's one for us to handle."

Too-reel ended the call on that note. *Deceive is going to be very hurt behind this one*, he thought. He knew the history between the two girls, and this wound would be deep.

*****

Everyone sat around a long table, awaiting Too-reel. No one

knew exactly what they were summoned there for except Ice. They were all talking amongst themselves when Too-reel walked in and took a seat at the head of the table. Everyone stopped talking and gave him their undivided attention.

"I know you all are wondering what we're doing here tonight. Yesterday, the money van was infiltrated. Fortunately, there were no funds in it at the time, which brings us here."

Everyone's faces at that moment twisted up in disbelief. They all looked a little confused. He went on before anyone could ask a question.

"Sonia, do you have something you would like to tell us?"

Sonia just held her head down in shame.

"Sonia, what the fuck is he talking about?" Deceive asked. Tears began to fall freely from Sonia's eyes.

"No, no, no. Say it ain't so!" Tabisha yelled.

"You fucking bitch!" Man yelled as she stood up.

"I'm going to leave this for you guys to handle, Deceive. Blue, Ice, Hype, let's go," Too-reel said.

The men all got up and left one by one, shaking their heads as they passed Sonia. Ice had a look of disgust on his face.

"Tashiba, Man, would you guys please wait outside?" Deceive asked.

"Fuck that! I want to hear what she's got to say," Man replied as she slung her chair.

"Please, Man. Let me handle this."

Man could see the pain and anguish in Deceive's eyes, so she fell back.

"After all we've been through." Man mushed Sonia in the back of the head as she walked by her. Tashiba looked at Sonia with tears in her eyes as she left the room.

"I'm sorry, Tashiba," Sonia muttered before Tashiba turned and walked away.

"Why, Sonia? Why?" Deceive asked.

"To protect you."

"To protect me from what?"

"From finding out the truth. I never meant to hurt you. They just wanted me to keep an eye on Too-reel."

"That doesn't make it any better. What kind of trouble were you in? What would make you do this in the first place? You know how we are."

"They used my past against me. I didn't want you to find out about me, about Bankroll." Sonia looked at Deceive with guilt in her face.

"Find out what? About my brother?"

"What we were doing. Bankroll was caught in the middle of a conspiracy, and I helped him do what he had to do. We were working for the government to stay on the streets." As Sonia spoke, more tears ran down her face.

"You're lying! You're fucking lying!" Deceive pulled her .38 from behind her back. She pointed it at Sonia with shaky hands as the tears started falling from her eyes.

"I didn't want you to find out like this. I never meant to hurt you."

"Shut up! I said, shut up!"

Block! Block! Block!

The three shots all struck Sonia in her chest.

"I love you, Tammie. Please don't hate me. I did it for you," Sonia said as her body slumped over and fell out of her chair and onto the floor. Deceive fell to her knees, crying.

Chapter 15

Babydoll sat inside a small room, handcuffed to a chair. She wondered why they had pulled her from her cell. She had already made it clear she wasn't about to cooperate with them. She knew it would be only a matter of time before Cruddy sent a lawyer once word got back from Bangout and Egypt that she had held it down.

Two agents entered the room. One held a small tape recorder in his hand. The other continued to stand by the door as the one with the tape recorder placed it on the table in front of Babydoll and pressed play.

At first, she didn't recognize the voices, but once the conversation continued, she knew it was Bangout and Cruddy, and they were talking in code. She listened to the tape for two minutes before she became very upset.

When the taped conversation was over, the line went dead, and the recording stopped. Babydoll hopped out of her seat.

"Fuck you, motherfucker! Fuck you!" she screamed like a mad woman at the tape recorder.

"Please calm down and take your seat, Ms. Hutson," one of the agents ordered.

"So that's how you play, huh?"

Babydoll continued to yell as she nodded repeatedly. She wasn't the least bit concerned with what the agent had said.

"OK, I can play dirty, too. I want to speak to Burgull. I'm not talking to no one else but him!" she demanded.

Burgull stood behind the one-way glass, watching as his hunch panned out. Burgull didn't have a clue about what they were talking about on the tape, but from his years of experience in the field, he knew how criminals' minds worked. He knew Babydoll had become a liability, and they were either going to leave her or get rid of her.

He hoped that one of the two options was mentioned in the taped conversation. The risk he had taken was about to pay off. He needed to move fast if he was going to catch the leader before he vanished.

"What's the rundown?"

"The guy who owned the shop said he didn't know what went down. He got a few gees and three free vehicles to keep his mouth shut," Ice replied.

"What were the three cars?" Too-reel asked.

"Our van, Rock's Benz, and the car the other guys drove."

"Yeah, some nigga they call Cruddy," Man said. "He said they had two other guys with him and a white female."

"If we can find out who this bitch is, we can find out more about this nigga. Dre said Rock met the bitch at Deceive's party. He said she was with another bad-looking Asian or Hispanic bitch."

"We need to find out who did this shit and fast. That's twice some niggas done disrespected us—first with my little cousin, and now with this. Next thing you know, everyone's going to want to try us," Ice said.

"I feel where you're coming from, and I want to get this shit cleared away as soon as possible so we can move on," Too-reel said.

Too-reel's cell phone rang. He screened the number before answering the call.

"Mick, what's up?"

"I got that thing you asked about. Why don't you drop by my office in an hour."

"I'm on my way." Too-reel clicked off the call. "Ice, I have got to make a quick run. I need you to stay on top of this shit. I've got a lot going on right now, and I can't count on no one else but you. Deceive's a little stuck behind that other shit."

"Yeah, but it was for the best. I'll hit you up when I'm through."

Too-reel threw on his helmet and hopped on his Ducati 1100 bike and sped off. It didn't take long for him to get to the Bronx on his bike. Mickey was waiting.

"Hey!" Mickey got up from his chair and gave Too-reel a bear hug. Mickey was a big guy, weighing over three hundred and fifty pounds, and standing six-feet-five inches. His stomach sat in his lap at all times, even when he stood.

"You're going to break my ribs, Mick," Too-reel said as Mickey released his hold.

"You need to stop by the house sometime and let Martha fix you some of her famous lasagna with stuffed sausage."

"How's Martha, by the way?"

"She's fine, you know. All she does is spend the money I bring home and bust my balls, but, hey, what am I going to do? I love the gal." Mickey and Too-reel shared a laugh.

"So, what's up, Mickey?" Too-reel got down to business.

"Come with me." Mickey led Too-reel to his office and closed the door along with his blinds. He then went to a painting on the wall and pulled it back, revealing a safe. After a few turns, the safe opened, and Mickey reached inside and pulled out a folder. He handed the folder to Too-reel before they sat down.

"It took a little work, but I got it. Here's the rundown on this guy. Jerol Pembroks Highmon came from a very wealthy family. His father was the CEO of a steel company out in LA, right. I mean, a huge company back then. They had contracts with everyone from the military to the airlines. But get this. His father was caught stealing money from the workers' pension plan. And since he wouldn't give up his accomplice, the stockholders pushed for the maximum sentence. The guy was sentenced to thirty years, and most of his assets were seized by the Feds.

"I did some more snooping, and I think the mob might have had their hands in that pension thing. But the guy couldn't talk or else his whole family might have been dead."

"Get the fuck out of here. You're telling me this rich son of a bitch took thirty years and didn't mention a word?"

"I'm telling you, it had to be the mob. But that's not where the drama comes in. According to the paperwork, Jerol had a sister that was being molested by their mother's boyfriend. There's a hidden report I practically had to dig up that says Jerol made a report to the cops, but his sister never admitted it was true."

"Shit! Didn't they check to see if it was true?"

"You've got to understand that they were only kids, and these were wealthy adults with influence and power. Who's going to believe them? It then goes on to say that Jerol was sent off to boarding school from when he was fourteen to eighteen. By the time he was twenty-three, he graduated from law school and had his first kid at twenty-seven by a Samantha Worthy. The baby was born with problems. The kid's retarded. It doesn't say too much about Jerol's mother except that she's in a nursing home. But that's another story.

"Now, get this. The name Highmon was his mother's maiden name before she got married to his father, which Jerol took on once his mother divorced his father. But his father's last name was Worthy," Mickey said with a wicked grin.

"So what?" Too-reel didn't see what Mickey was trying to tell him.

"So what? Jerol's father had a daughter before he married his mother."

"He was fucking his own sister?"

"Exactly! She still lives in LA in an old family mansion. She's on medication. They say she's not all there."

"What about the kid?"

"Oh, he's there, too. The staff looks after them. Jerol takes a trip out west every few months to check on them. I also spoke with one of the maids. She said if she didn't know any better, she would think the kid was Jerol's by the way he treats him."

"So they really don't know that's his son?"

"He's still covering up dirt. With the mother in a home, and the sister considered to be crazy, who else's word do they have to go on but his?"

"This motherfucker's sick!"

"Lifestyle of the rich and famous," Mickey replied with a chuckle.

"Thanks a lot, Mickey. This is for your troubles." Too-reel handed Mickey an envelope stuffed with hundred-dollar bills.

"No problem, guy. Anytime."

Mickey shook his hand. Too-reel took the folder and placed it under his armpit before he left. *Time to even out the playing field*, he thought as he walked out of Mickey's place.

*****

Babydoll had told Burgull every piece of information she knew about Cruddy and agreed to testify against him when they caught him. She made it seem like she and the other girls were forced into setting up guys or Cruddy would have killed them. She also gave up a few other robberies. She was then granted a visit, and her older sister Rachel came to see her.

"What the fuck's up, sis?" Rachel asked.

"This motherfucker was going to just leave me for dead. After all I did for his bitch ass!" Babydoll replied into the receiver as she looked at her sister through the glass window.

"I told you about that trifling-ass nigga! I knew he wasn't shit."

Rachel was just mad that Cruddy had chosen Babydoll over her because she looked younger and better.

"And that nigga Cutter, I got something for his ass."

"What did he do?"

"He was filling Cruddy's head with bullshit about me. But fuck that. You trying to make some money or what?" Babydoll knew damn well money was all Rachel lived for. She would get it any way she could—fuck, suck, whatever.

"Hell yeah. I'm trying to get paid."

"A'ight, check this. You know that nigga Ice and his crew that be uptown all the time?"

"Who don't know them niggas! Shit, they getting that feddi!"

"Look, Ice's cousin was the one who got killed at Club New York a few months back."

"Oh yeah? I remember that shit was jumping."

"Anyway, Ice is offering fifty gees to anyone who can lead him to the killers. All you have to do is call him and tell him what I'm about to tell you. I'll give you fifteen gees out of the money."

"Damn, just fifteen? Why don't we split it down the middle?"

"How about you don't get shit, and I'll find someone else to do this?" Babydoll stared at her greedy sister.

"I was just playing anyway. Damn, bitch!" Rachel rolled her eyes.

"Look, get him to come by the house tonight and bring the money with him. I'm going to call at eight on the dot. Let him know I'm going to give him the name and address of the killer. That way we don't have to get into too much detail over the phone. And make sure Mama is there."

"Why?"

"Because I don't trust you with my money. That's why!"

"Whatever."

****

Eight PM

Ice was at Babydoll's mother's apartment with Rachel, waiting for the call. Sure enough, it came at eight. Rachel answered and accepted it before handing the phone to Ice.

"Yo!"

"His name is Cutter, and his mother lives at 112 Linden Boulevard. You can catch him there at any given time. He's brown-skinned with a low cut."

"Shorty, why would I believe you when you're where you're at?"

"They shitted on me, so fuck them! I know what you're about, and if anything happens, you're at my mother's house, and I love my mother. You feel me now?"

"I'll take that."

"One more thing. My sister only gets fifteen. Give the rest to my moms. She'll make sure I get it." Ice passed the phone back to Rachel.

"Yeah?" Rachel asked.

"Where's Mom at?" Babydoll asked.

"She's right here."

"Tell her I'll call her back in thirty minutes."

"OK." Rachel hung up. "She said for you to give me the money," Rachel told Ice. Rachel stuck out her palm.

Ice sucked his teeth and took fifteen gees out of the bag and threw it to her. "Where's your mother at?" he asked.

"Mom!" Rachel yelled. A woman in her early fifties came from the back bedroom.

"Why are you screaming like that, Rachel?"

"Good evening, ma'am. Your daughter told me to give you this."

"He handed her the book bag that he carried with the remaining money. She took the bag and looked at it strangely.

"Ma, it's from Laren," Rachel said.

"She said you would know what to do with it," Ice said as he got up to leave.

"Thank you, young man."

"So, Ice, what are you doing later?" Rachel asked as she walked him to the door. He was about to blow her off until he saw a picture on the wall with four girls in it. The white girl in the photo stood out the most.

"Who's this?" he pointed.

"Oh, that's just Cocaine, one of Babydoll's friends."

Ice took a closer look and noticed the Spanish-looking Asian girl. *This must be who Dre was talking about*, he thought.

"Do you know these girls?" Ice asked.

"Not really," Rachel said with an attitude, thinking Ice wanted to hook up with one of them.

"I was just trying to find out something. If you can locate shorty right here for me, I'll not only take you out, but I'll give you another fifteen gees."

"A'ight!" Rachel jumped at the thought of making more money.

"Let me get this picture right here," Ice said as he took the framed photo off the wall before he exited the apartment.

Chapter 16

Burgull was on his way home when he stopped at an Amoco to pick up some beer and cigarettes.

"Where the fuck did this weather come from?" he asked himself as he threw his jacket over his head and hopped out of the truck. He ran inside the store before he got too wet from the downpour.

Ding, dong!

The doorbell rang as he came through it.

"Hey, Charley," he said to the clerk as he headed toward the back of the store to the cooler.

"Looks like we got ourselves a nasty one today, huh?" Charley shouted from behind the counter.

"Tell me about it!" Burgull yelled as he grabbed two six-packs of Budweiser. He then headed back up front to the counter.

As he approached, Charley reached up and got down two packs of Marlboros. "What? No snack tonight?" he asked as he rang up the items.

"No, not tonight. Ann wants me to watch my cholesterol. I'm out here fighting bad guys all day, and she's worried about my cholesterol killing me," Burgull told him as he pulled out some cash from his wallet to pay for his items.

Burgull and the clerk both laughed as Burgull paid him.

"See you tomorrow," Charley said as he gave Burgull his change with his beer and cigarettes in a plastic shopping bag. Burgull threw the jacket back over his head as he ran back out into the rain.

When he got back inside the truck, he placed the bag on the passenger seat and shook off the chills that ran through his body. He then reached inside the bag and grabbed a pack of Marlboros. He opened it, got out a cigarette, and lit it before pulling off. The rain was coming down so hard, Burgull could barely see the traffic as he attempted to pull onto the streets. He looked to his left and right as he eased his foot off the brake, letting the truck slowly roll into the street.

Wham!

Someone ran into the front of his truck from the side.

"Oh, shit!"

The cigarette fell from his lips, into his lap. The fire started to burn a hole straight through his pants and onto his leg.

"Aahhh!"

He hopped up as he began to brush the ashes from his lap by slapping his leg. After turning off his vehicle, Burgull stepped out into the rain to check out the damage and make sure no one was hurt.

"Oh my God! I'm so sorry. I didn't see you pulling out!" the young lady said with her hands over her mouth.

"Calm down, ma'am. I'm fine. Is anyone else in the car with you?"

"No. Are you hurt? Is there anyone else with you?" the lady asked.

"No, there's no one else with me. Do you have insurance with you?"

"Yes, yes, I do."

"May I please see it?"

"Wait a minute. I'm going to have to see yours, too."

"How about you get yours and I'll get mine. Is that fine with you?"

"Sure."

As Burgull was heading back to his truck, he could have sworn he had met this woman before. He searched through his memory until it came to him. Yes, she was one of the girls he took a picture with in front of the jewelry store, and the one they'd picked up was with her, too. That was when he remembered they said they had been following him.   He reached inside his jacket to retrieve his gun from his shoulder holster, then spun back around.

Bloc! Bloc! Bloc! Bloc! Bloc!

All five shots connected with Burgull's chest.

Bup! Bup! Bup!

Burgull managed to squeeze off a few rounds of his own before he fell backward. China was kneeling on the pavement next to her car with her hands over her ears. Wolf looked down at her before he fell to his knees, and then onto his face, gun still in hand.

Burgull was still moving, trying to get to his gun that had fallen out of his hand when he fell. Cruddy walked over to him, kicking the gun out of his reach.

"You should have stayed out of my business!"

Blop! Blop! Blop! Blop! Blop!

Cruddy shot him five more times in the face before they both made it to the van that was parked behind the crashed car, leaving Wolf's body laid out in the middle of the street. Cruddy didn't even check to see if he was still alive.

"Drive!" he said to D-Range as he pulled out from behind the car, running over Wolf's body.

Cutter pulled up in front of his mother's house and parked. He threw the car into park so fast, it caused the car to rock forward as it stopped. He hopped out and ran to the door, inserting his key and turning the lock, then pushing the door open. He ran inside and closed the door behind him, then took off up the stairs. He ran to his room and went straight to his closet. He grabbed a small bag and started loading some clothes in it, along with two guns and boxes of bullets. He reached under his bed and pulled out a Timberland shoebox. When he opened it, stacks of money stared back at him. He took out twenty stacks and threw them into his bag with the clothes and zipped it up. He took the shoebox with him as he headed back downstairs.

"Boy, what's your hurry?" his mother asked when he came running down the steps.

"Ma, I have to go!"

"Oh, Lord, what have you done this time?"

"I haven't done anything, Ma. Here. There's some money in here I want you to keep."

"Boy, you know I'm not taking any drug money from you."

"This is not any drug money, Ma. I earned this money on my own."

"Doing God knows what." Cutter's mother rolled her eyes and sucked her teeth.

"Would you just listen to me and stop talking for a minute? I want you to have this. You deserve to live better. I'm tired of seeing you live from hand to mouth, working to pay bills. I want you to get yourself something nice or go somewhere you always wanted to go. I can't stay here any longer."

Cutter could see the pleading look for more answers in his mother's eyes. He didn't allow her to speak.

"Please believe me when I say I didn't do it. No matter what people say. I'm sorry for screaming at you, but I've got to go."

Cutter gave his mother a brief hug and kiss on the cheek. As he was getting ready to leave, a news flash on the living room TV caught his eye.

"This just in. A New York federal agent was gunned down just blocks away from his New Jersey home today. Eyewitnesses say what seemed to be a car accident turned into a deadly shooting that left two dead. The FBI released a statement saying it was no accident, but a planned ambush and execution. The name of the high-ranking agent has not been released to the public because the family has not yet been notified. Please stay tuned for more on this breaking story."

The TV screen switched to an overhead view of the location and the crime scene. There were police cars all over the streets with flashing lights. Agents in FBI jackets, along with local police were on sight, combing the place. Yellow crime-scene tape ran from corner to corner, blocking off the main scene.

Cutter knew exactly who it was and what had gone down. He took one last look at his mother before taking off out the door. Cutter's mother stood there looking at the TV as she wondered what her son had gotten into. He was moving so fast, she had forgotten to tell him someone had stopped by looking for him thirty minutes ago.

Cutter ran to the trunk of his car and pressed the button, causing it to pop open as he dropped his bag into it and closed it. He ran around to the driver's side and was opening the door when someone called his name.

"Yo, Cutter!" a voice yelled from behind him. As soon as Cutter turned around, he was greeted by a hail of bullets. He didn't even get a chance to see his assailant as everything faded to black.

Cutter's mother heard the gunshots, followed by sounds of screeching car tires before she ran to the door and opened it. She saw a green car speeding away. She didn't have to see her son's body to know what had just happened. She felt it in her heart as she fell to the floor on her knees and started weeping.

"You think he's alive?"

"Come on. I know I hit him up at least six to ten times, all upper body," Ice replied.

"Shit, I caught him a few times, too, in the face. These .44 shots ain't no joke, either. Even if he had on a vest or a helmet, that shit's going straight through," Hitman said.

"That's for Reggie. Now we got to find these other niggas and that bitch that robbed us."

"That's a bad little white bitch in that picture. I see why she had Rock fucked up. But, man, that Asian-looking bitch is even worse."

"Hell yeah. I ain't even going to front. I wouldn't mind hitting that before we kill them."

"Man, you're a cold motherfucker!" Hitman said as he let out a chuckle.

"That's what they call me."

"He's not answering his phone, Daddy," Cocaine said as she, China, and Cruddy sat in the Expedition.

"He knows what time it is. I'm not waiting any longer. Let's go. Them niggas on their own."

Cocaine pulled out of the gas station, heading toward I-95 South on the Jersey Turnpike with D-Range tailing them.

Chapter 17

"This just in. We can now release the name of the federal agent who was gunned down just blocks from his New Jersey home. Director Theodore Burgull." A photograph of Burgull in his uniform appeared on the screen.

"Ooooh, shit!" Bangout shouted as he hopped up from his couch in front of the TV. "Egypt, we've got to get the fuck out of here right now!" Bangout raced to his living room window and peeked outside from behind his blinds. *Good*, he thought as he spotted the gray Impala parked down the block from his apartment.

"What's wrong?"

Egypt emerged from the bathroom in a pair of jeans and a bra. She had a towel wrapped around her head.

"What's wrong! This dumb motherfucker went and killed a federal agent. It's just a matter of time before they scoop us up. This shit's serious!"

"What?" Egypt was confused. Bangout was talking too fast. When she looked at the TV and saw the headline, along with the aerial shot, she quickly figured it out.

"You better hurry the fuck up and come on. They're still out front. We'll take the back window." Bangout grabbed his motorcycle keys and a knapsack from the closet. He knew if he could make it to his bike parked around the block, he could give them a run for their money or die trying.

"But we're on the second floor!" Egypt replied.

"You can stay if you want to. I'm gone." Bangout headed to his kitchen and opened the window.

"I'm coming. Don't leave me!" Egypt ran into the bedroom and put on her sneakers. She grabbed one of Bangout's shirts from the closet. Bangout threw the bag out the window before he jumped.

When he landed, he felt the bottom of his feet sting from the impact of the jump. He then picked up the bag and looked up at Egypt looking through the window. Egypt was hesitant when she began to climb out of the window. She backed out as she held on to the edge of the window and let herself hang.

"I'm scared, Bangout," she mumbled.

"Just let go. I got you." Bangout positioned himself underneath her and prepared for her to fall.

"I . . . I . . . I can't," Egypt mumbled again, this time sounding like she was about to cry.

"Yo, I'm going to leave you if you don't come the fuck on already." Egypt was about to climb inside when she heard a loud knock coming from Bangout's front door. She instantly let go and fell on her feet before falling to her butt.

"Aahh! I think I twisted my leg." When Egypt tried to get up, she couldn't stand up straight on one of her legs. Bangout placed his arm around her back to support her from falling as they took off. With every step Egypt took, she limped and hopped.

It wasn't long before the police kicked in Bangout's door and charged into the apartment. After checking all the rooms, they realized he had gotten away.

"In here," one of the officers shouted.

"They must have gone out the window," one of the agents said as he stuck his head through the window to scan the area. He had no clue where they might have gone. All he heard was the roaring engine of a motorcycle in the distance.

*****

"I hate fucking with these simple-minded bitches," Ice said as he pressed send and placed the cell phone to his ear.

"Hello?"

"What's up, ma? Did you find her for me?"

"I can't find that bitch. Nobody knows where she's at, not even her mother," Rachel replied.

"Next time you talk to your sister, ask her what she can tell me about a guy named Cruddy."

"Cruddy? I know Cruddy!"

"What do you know about him?"

"I can tell you over dinner."

"Listen, shorty, this is not the time to be fucking around, a'ight!"

"Dag, I was just playing. You didn't have to act like that." Rachel sucked her teeth.

"My bad, shorty. I'm under a lot of pressure right now. I'm going to holler at you, and who knows, maybe you can help get rid of some of this stress." Ice knew what kind of bitch Rachel was, and he wasn't ready to run her away yet.

"Maybe. I'll think about it. Call me when you get downstairs."

"Stinking-ass bitch!" Ice yelled when he hung up the phone and looked at Hitman.

"You're a hard man to keep up with," Deceive said as she strolled into Too-reel's office.

"Hey, Deceive. How're you doing?"

"I'm doing good now."

Deceive walked up to him and wrapped her hands around his neck, trying to kiss him on the lips, but he turned his head to the side, and she kissed him on his cheek instead.

Knock! Knock!

Two knocks came from the door before it was opened and Vanessa walked in.

"Ooh, I didn't know you had company." Vanessa saw Deceive with her arms wrapped around Too-reel's neck, and her face inches away from his. Tears filled her eyes as she turned and slammed the door.

"Vanessa!" Too-reel pushed Deceive away from him and went after Vanessa.

"Let her go!" Deceive grabbed his hand. He snatched it back and ran through the door. Deceive had a wicked smile on her face.

By the time he reached the elevator, the door had just closed with Vanessa behind it. He took off for the stairs, hoping to beat the elevator down to the parking garage. He made it to the parking level, out of breath, just in time to see Vanessa heading to her car. Once she saw him, she started to run as she fumbled through her purse for her car keys. By the time she hit the button on her keychain and grabbed the handle to the car door, pulling it open, Too-reel pushed the door shut.

"No! No! No! Just let me go!" Vanessa began to pound on his chest. He grabbed her in a bear hug and tried to calm her down.

"It wasn't what it seemed."

"You're lying. I know about you and her, Terell!" Vanessa

continued to twist from side to side, trying to break loose from Too-reel. "Get off me! Let me go!"

"I'm not going to let you go until I say what I have to say, so you're going to have to calm down." A man was heading to his car but stopped to see what all the commotion was about. "Mind your fucking business!" Too-reel yelled at the man as he took off with a quickness. "I told you it wasn't what it seemed."

"Then what was it, huh? I saw the pictures, Terell. Jerol showed me the pictures."

"What pictures?"

"The ones with you and her in the hotel on your little trip!" Too-reel held his head down.

"That's what I thought."

Vanessa tried to shake free again.

"I told you I was sorry for the way things turned out. I tried to do everything to prove to you I love you, but I'm not about to stand by and let you dog me out and use me, Terell!" Tears rolled down her cheeks as she spoke.

"Is that what you think I'm doing, using you? Yes, what you saw in the pictures was true, Vanessa, but I only did that for one reason, and one reason only. After what I found out about you, I was destroyed emotionally. Here was the one person I loved, next to my mother, and she turns out to be an undercover cop, sent to bring me down. My pride and my first instinct was to squeeze the life out of you and watch you die a slow death. And as much as I hated you, my heart still overshadowed those feelings.

"Deceive let me know how she had been feeling toward me, and I kind of felt like she was the next perfect match for me. So, I had to sleep with her in order to know how deep these feelings I have for you run. I feel bad for using her now, but I know I'm willing to do anything to try to fix this thing between me and you . . . I mean us."

He placed his arm on her stomach and looked deep into her eyes. "I was just about to let Deceive know that what happened between us was a mistake and could never take place again because I'm already in love with someone else. I've swallowed my pride and accepted these feelings I have for you."

Vanessa was speechless. All she could do was look at him as he poured his heart out.

"Baby, we can get past this."

"You promise?" Vanessa asked as she buried her face in his chest.

"I promise." Too-reel hugged her tightly.

Deceive stood in a far corner of the parking lot, listening to their conversation. She was distraught as a teardrop rolled down the side of her face.

"I'm going to get that cop bitch!"

Chapter 18

As Ice drove down 125th Street in Harlem, he suddenly swerved into the oncoming lane. He grabbed the steering wheel and swerved back into his lane just as two cars on the opposite lane flew past him, their horns blaring.

"That's enough!" he yelled.

This bitch's mouth was good for more than just talking. She would give Superhead a run for her money, he thought as Rachel's head emerged from his lap as she wiped off the corner of her mouth.

"Sorry."

Rachel knew what he was doing. Her head game was some of the best in the city. Niggas' car insurance were known to go up for fucking with her.

"Did you holler at your sister for me about the thing?"

"Yeah, I spoke to her. She said for you to stay away from him because the Feds want him for murdering one of their directors. She said they're holding his mother and sister for questioning."

Fuck, Ice thought. He wanted to send a little message to Cruddy through his family, but it was going to be hard now with the Feds keeping an eye on them.

"Did you get that other thing I asked you for?"

"Oh, here you go." She handed Ice a picture with Babydoll and Cruddy on the beach. Cruddy had on sunglasses and a visor.

"I don't think I know him."

"That nigga's on the low key. If he don't know you from when y'all was kids, he's not going to fuck with you. All him and his goons do is rob people for a living," Rachel replied as she smacked on her chewing gum.

"Is that right?" Ice decided he was going to continue to fuck with Rachel for information purposes only. She was a real hood rat, and one thing a hood rat was good for was knowing what was going on in the hood before it hit the press.

Vanessa and Too-reel were just leaving the condo when they were approached by four agents.

"Agent Tyson, would you please come with us?" one of the agents asked as he flashed his badge.

"What is this all about? Do you know what you guys are doing?" Vanessa asked, a little confused.

"You've been called in. Now would you please come with us, now!" Two of the agents stood on each side of Vanessa, and Too-reel was about to intervene.

"No, I'll go with them." Vanessa stopped Too-reel. The agents escorted her to a black SUV and pulled off, leaving Too-reel standing outside.

Vanessa was taken to the same office building where the interrogation had taken place. She was escorted to an office where Jerol sat waiting.

"What's going on, Jerol?" she demanded as soon as she came through the door.

"I'm pulling you out. You're no longer on this case. You will be escorted to the airport where a ticket will be waiting for you in your real name. I expect you to use it. You've been transferred to a new office in LA, along with your promotion and a new place that's been set up for you."

"No! I'm not ready to leave. Why now?"

"It's become clear to me you are no longer capable of making rational decisions. Point blank, your emotions have gotten involved and you cannot and will not be trusted any longer."

"That's bullshit, Jerol! What's the real reason you're doing this? Or is this just another part of your game?" Vanessa was furious.

"Games? I assure you this is not a game, Agent Tyson. I appreciate your work, but now it's time to say goodbye. Gentlemen, would you please escort Agent Tyson to the airport? She has a flight to catch. And one more thing, if you make any contact with Mr. Cobe, I'll not only have your badge, but I'll be the one to personally prosecute you. And you wouldn't like that."

"You used me! You used me!" Vanessa yelled as she was escorted out of his office.

"Yes, my dear, we are all used at one point or another."

"Yo!" Too-reel answered his phone, sounding a little agitated. He was tailing the black Yukon that held Vanessa.

"Is this a bad time to call you?"

"No, my bad, Tashiba. I didn't mean to sound like that toward you."

"You want me to call you back?"

"Nah, I'm good. What's up?"

"Well, you know Deceive's been under a lot of stress and she's paranoid since that shit with Sonia, right?"

Where the fuck is she going with this? he wondered. *I hope Deceive ain't on no kiddie shit by having Tashiba calling me for her. I don't got time for this shit.*

"I thought I overheard her say something about Vanessa being the police. At first, I wasn't going to pay it no attention, but I figured I'd tell you anyway so you could look into it. Better safe than sorry, know what I mean?"

"Yeah, I think I'll do that. Thanks for the heads up, Tashiba. By the way, where is Deceive right now?"

"She went somewhere. She didn't even bother to tell a bitch. I hope she snaps out of this shit soon, you know."

"Deceive is a strong woman. She'll be a'ight."

"I hope so," Tashiba said in a sad voice.

"I'll holler at you later, Tash."

"Bye."

After Tashiba hung up, Too-reel began to wonder how the fuck Deceive found out about Vanessa. *Did she overhear us in the parking garage? But I left her inside my office. I've got to wrap this thing up before it gets out of hand.*

Too-reel's thoughts were interrupted. "JFK? Why the fuck are they taking her to the airport?" he said out loud as he continued to tail the black Yukon.

Too-reel picked up his cell and made a phone call. The call was quick and to the point as he said, "Keep a watch on her." After his brief statement, he pulled away and headed to his next destination.

Brody exited the hospital room with a smile across his face. He pulled out his cell phone and placed a call.

"What do you have for me, Agent Brody?"

"Just like you said, he's ready to cut a deal and testify against Too-reel if it comes down to it. He also knows how their operation is run."

"We already have all the information we need on him, so see who else he can give up."

"OK, Jerol. I'll call you back as soon as I'm finished here." Brody wasn't surprised at how many cases they had built and were still building off Grimy and Pockets alone. It was like a domino effect. One fall brought more down with them.

Rock was now one of the third bosses out of Too-reel's five-person deadly venom crew who was ready to cooperate. Two more and they would have everyone.

As cold as some of these individuals were, they were cowards when it came to pulling the time. They were all willing to tell on the one who was feeding them. Too-reel was just the bait for them. Once they bit, they would tell everything else, too. The snitch virus was spreading rapidly on the streets. Brody opened the door leading back to Rock's room.

"Can I get you a smoke?" he asked as he returned to Rock's room.

Chapter 19

"Yeah, young nigga, I told you I would get you paid. This is my block now."

"Damn, Grimy, how did you know them niggas would get knocked?"

"It was just a matter of time, li'l man. Them niggas been had their turn." Grimy took a pull of his blunt as he leaned on his new BMW 745 in a cocky stance.

"Oh, here comes them niggas I told you was looking for you earlier." A green Grand Cherokee with tinted windows pulled up and stopped next to the BMW as the driver's side window rolled down.

"Yo, anyone seen Grimy?" the driver asked.

"Who want to know?" Grimy positioned himself by the car door as he reached behind him and grabbed the handle to his gun.

"We just need to holla at him, that's all, cuz."

"About what?" Grimy asked defensively.

"About his snitch ass!"

An arm came around Grimy's shoulder, and he saw the flash of the orange boxcutter as it slid across his neck. Instantly, Grimy grasped his neck as he turned around to see the same little man he was talking to earlier, clutching the boxcutter in his hand.

"That's for my cousin, you bitch-ass nigga."

The kid spat in Grimy's face. The driver of the Jeep hopped out with a .38 in his hand. He walked up to Grimy and shot him twice in the back of his head before returning to the Jeep and pulling off with the young kid in the backseat.

A small group of guys stood on the corner of the block, watching the whole thing unfold. Everyone knew what Grimy was doing, but no one said shit because he was a live wire and had money. They didn't care because it wasn't their people he'd told on, but as soon as it was one of theirs who did the telling, it was do what you've got to do. Yeah, the game was funny like that—at least the players were.

"Hi, Too-reel. It's nice to see you."

"Thanks for seeing me, Tanya. I appreciate you calling me."

"I don't know what's wrong with him, but I know you would never do anything to get him into any trouble. I know you were one of the few friends he had."

Tanya looked at Too-reel as if she was about to start tearing up at any moment.

"Well, whatever it is he did, I'm pretty sure he had a good reason for doing it." Too-reel pulled out a stack of bills and handed them to her.

"I'm not doing this for the money. I just hate he sold you out." Tanya didn't accept the money right away.

"I want you to have this, Tanya. You're a good girl." Too-reel placed the money in her lap. She covered it with both her palms.

"I don't know what happened to him. He's been coming home every other night now that it seems he's making a little more money. He leaves drugs out all over the house like he doesn't have a care in the world. He's even fucking that bitch next door." Tanya broke down in tears. *That's the real reason you called me*, Too-reel thought as he looked at Tanya with sympathy.

"He's upstairs, right?"

"Yes."

"By himself?"

"Yes. I told him I was just running to the corner store. Please don't hurt him."

"I'm not going to do anything to him. I just want to talk to him. That's all."

"The apartment is 1811. This key is for the top lock. The other one's for the bottom." Tanya gave him her set of keys.

"Don't worry. I'll be gone by the time you return, and I won't hurt him," he repeated.

"I know you won't."

Too-reel exited his truck and made it across the street to the building. He walked into the lobby and took the stairs to the second floor. He walked down the hallway until he spotted 1811 on a brown door.

He slowly inserted the first key into the top lock. He turned it slowly as he turned the knob and pushed the door open. It didn't budge. He then inserted the second key into the bottom lock and turned it. This time, when he turned the knob and pushed the door, it opened. He slowly opened the door and stepped inside before closing it behind him. He took his gun from his waist as he looked around. He heard music coming from a bedroom toward the back. He headed toward the music with caution.

"What the fuck took you so long, Tany?" a voice shouted from the back room. "I hope you brought me back something to eat!"

As Too-reel got closer to the bedroom, he smelled something similar to plastic being burned with weed. He saw Pockets in the room in his boxers and no shirt, playing a PSP.

"Don't you hear me talking to you? What the fuck's your—" Pockets' heart jumped out of his chest when he glanced back and saw Too-reel standing in the doorway. He immediately dropped the remote control, along with the blunt.

"What's up, Pockets? I've been trying to reach you for a while now."

"Ha, Too-reel! I've been trying to reach you for a while now."

"Cut the bullshit, Pockets! All I want to know is why. Why did you flip so quick? You know I got you."

"Got me, all right. Got me fucked up. That's what you got me. You were the only one that got me screwed."

"What the fuck are you talking about?"

"That shit with Grimy!"

"So instead of letting me know, you sold me out, and who knows who else! After all the shit we've been through!"

"Man, you don't know what it feels like to be locked up. They make you feel like you ain't shit, like you're less than a man." Pockets kept his eyes on the gun in Too-reel's hand.

"So you feel like a man for selling out your people?" Too-reel could see the gun was making Pockets nervous, so he tucked it back into his waist.

"I . . . I couldn't see myself doing any more time. Not with my girl out here on her own. They didn't even want you. I gave them some other guys from White Plains. They said they already knew about you."

"You know how I feel about that shit, Pockets. I would have

done anything for you. We grew up together. Your moms is like my mother. We slept in the same bed, wore the same clothes."

"Come on, Terell. Look at you and look at me. You live good as fuck while I'm still in the hood."

"Whose fault is that? How many times have I tried to help you out, not even on no street-level shit. I bought your mother her house."

"Yeah, I'm a fucking grown man. I don't want no other nigga taking care of me like I'm his bitch! I don't need no fucking handout. I'm a fucking man, too, you know! You always had shit better!"

Too-reel couldn't believe the shit Pockets was saying. It was like he resented him for the longest time and was finally letting it out. As Too-reel stared at him, he noticed a few crushed up rocks on the dresser next to some weed. He looked back at Pockets.

"Yeah, I'm smoking now," Pockets said.

Too-reel just shook his head and turned to walk away.

"Yeah, nigga, we all can't be diehard niggas like you, Mr. Big Shot! Fuck you, nigga! Fuck you!"

Too-reel exited the apartment, closing the door behind him.

Pockets knocked over everything inside the room as he went into a tantrum. He broke the TV and the huge dresser mirror before falling to his knees, crying.

After leaving the Bronx, Too-reel drove to his mother's house and parked in his usual spot two houses down. He let himself in with his set of keys and walked to the living room, where his mother sat, watching her soaps. He gave her a kiss on the cheek before sitting down next to her. He watched TV with her for two hours until she finally spoke.

"Terell, is there something you would like to tell me?"

Too-reel looked at his mother's aging face and smiled. She always seemed to know when something was bothering him. She knew him so well.

He took a deep breath.

"Ma, you know you're the most important person in my life, and I would do anything in this world for you, including give up my life."

"Terell, why are you talking like that?"

"Ma, just hear me out, please. You single-handedly raised me from a boy into the man I am today. I know I might not have headed in the direction you wanted for me, but nevertheless, you accept me for who I am. Ma, Vanessa's pregnant and she wants us to start a family, but—"

"But what, Terell? Wouldn't you like a family of your own, sweetheart?"

"Yes, but my lifestyle."

"Well, change it."

"I'm afraid I can't. I'm in too deep."

"That's nonsense, boy. You can change if you really want to."

"It's not that easy, Ma. There's a lot of things I'm not telling you. I don't want to leave a child in this world without me being there for him. I've watched you struggle too hard to make the same mistake my sperm donor made."

"You cannot compare yourself to that man, Terell. You are nothing like him. I know you wouldn't run out on your family."

"But that's what I'll be doing if I end up in prison or dead."

"Terell, you can only control what you can. The rest is in the Lord's hands. You cannot be afraid to live your life. We all have a path we must walk."

"Ma, no disrespect, but the Lord cannot help me. These people don't care about the Lord. They're not playing fair. We don't live by God's laws, we live by man's laws."

"No, you live by man's laws, Terell. They can only do what you allow them to do. I don't want you to worry about me. I will be all right by the will of the Lord. You have some demons within you that you need to let go of, Terell. Stop holding on to the past. Free yourself from these burdens. Stop running these streets and settle down with Vanessa. Maybe her having this baby is a sign from God. Listen to it, Terell."

Too-reel looked his mother deep in her brown eyes. He knew then he could never explain the situation he was caught up in and have her understand. She had no clue as to how dirty these people played. These were the same people who had crucified her so-called Lord and Savior, Jesus Christ.

Instead of continuing to try to explain why he was about to do what he was about to do, he reached inside his pocket and produced a white envelope and handed it to her.

"What is this?"

"Inside are the deeds to my buildings. Inside the building on the third floor, Apartment D, there are two safes located in the kitchen walls. The code to the safes is in there also. There are also two more codes in there. They're for my offshore accounts. The number for my lawyer is also in there. If you have any questions or problems, ask him. He's the one who got everything set up for me. Vanessa will know what to do with the money in the safe. I want you to know I love you and would never hurt you intentionally."

Too-reel leaned forward and kissed his mother on her cheeks before getting up and leaving. Ms. Cobe sat in the same spot, gazing at the wall, knowing she might never see her son alive again.

"May the Lord be with you, my son," she whispered as a tear ran from the corner of her eye.

Chapter 20

Jerol sat comfortably in the upstairs den of the house as he puffed on a Cuban cigar and sipped a glass of warm Scotch. His attention was drawn to the door as he heard someone approaching.

He was curious who it might be because he wasn't expecting anyone else. His other colleagues knew he was using the house, and they wouldn't dare show up unannounced. *It must be Brody*, he thought, *but how did he get inside? I must have left the door unlocked.*

"I'm in the den, Brody!"

The footsteps got closer as someone stopped in front of the door. The handle on the door slowly turned, and the door opened. Jerol nearly choked on his cigar when he saw whose face appeared from behind the door. He sat straight up in the soft leather chair as he tried to keep his composure.

"Mr. Cobe, what are you doing here? I hope this is a life-or-death matter because my office hours are from eight to five."

Jerol's mind raced, wondering how Too-reel knew where this house was, but most of all, how he had gotten inside. He wondered if his accomplice had set him up.

As Too-reel stepped inside, he closed the door behind him, leaving it cracked as he approached Jerol. He noticed the two glasses of Scotch as he took a seat across from Jerol.

"I see you were expecting company."

"Mr. Cobe, you're running my patience thin. I hope you know what you have just done to your mother."

Too-reel threw the yellow envelope he had in his hand onto the desk. Jerol placed his cigar into a huge, round crystal ashtray and picked up the envelope. As soon as he opened it, a photo of his retarded son fell onto the desk. Jerol snatched it up and stared at it before looking back at Too-reel. He then began digging through the rest of the envelope. He saw another picture of his son being fed at the house in California, along with another picture of his sister in the garden, seated in a chair, rocking back and forth. There was a picture of his mother at the nursing home, and two pictures of Jerol's father, along with the article that was printed on the day of his sentencing.

Jerol's face turned beet red as he looked back over the pictures, not believing what he was seeing. He threw the pictures back down on the desk.

"How dare you!" he roared.

"No. You fuck with my family, and I fuck with yours. I know all about you and your family's secrets. Your son from your own sister? You disgust me, walking around here like you're better than me when your father was just like me."

"You know nothing about my father! I have no father. Don't you mention that man. He's nothing to me. He disgraced his family." For a moment, Too-reel felt like he and Jerol were riding in the same boat.

"No, you are the disgrace. How would your peers look at you now if they found out your sister is the mother of your child, and your father died behind bars because he wouldn't cooperate?"

"Shut up! You know nothing! Shut up! All he had to do was give them up, and he would have been home to watch me and my sister grow up. He would have been there to make sure we didn't get raped. It's all his fault. All we had was each other. I loved her, and she loved me!"

Jerol had to catch himself. His emotions were spiraling out of control. He quickly calmed down, ran his fingers through his hair, and straightened out his smoker's jacket. "Please forgive me for my outburst," Jerol said. "Touché, it looks like you have gained the upper hand. The ball is in your court."

"You are going to forget about my mother. If a squad car so much as drives by her house too slowly, you will know how it feels to have your loved ones held accountable for your actions. There's a million dollars on your nephew slash son and your sister slash baby's mother. I don't think your mother has very long to live, but just in case, there will be a bullet with her name, too. I also have the addresses of a few good journalists that would love this story. Don't try to move your family because I have copies of your and your sister's DNA, along with hospital records. I also have more copies of that front-page article. You can keep those."

Too-reel got up to leave as Jerol sat glued to his seat. Before Too-reel walked out the door, he turned back around.

"Checkmate."

He had used Jerol's own strategy to beat him. He turned to leave.

POW! POW! POW!

A bullet struck Too-reel in his back while one hit him in the shoulder, sending him falling to the ground, pushing the door wide open. When he rolled over onto his back and looked up, he saw a shadow emerging from behind the long curtains, pointing a gun at him.

"It's not going to end like that."

The voice was very familiar to Too-reel. Then, the face came into view.

"Surprised to see me? I knew you were getting weak behind that bitch."

"De . . . Deceive. What are you doing?"

"I tried to tell you, but you wouldn't listen. We could have run this town together, but you wanted to be with that slut bitch even when you found out she was a cop. All you had to do was give up some of those petty hustlers, and everything would have been just fine!"

"So it was you the whole time, not Sonia. You got my mother involved."

"Yes, it was me. I used Sonia after I found out her location to make her look like the leak. I'm the one that told them about your mother and helped seal the deal with those accounts I had set up in her name. Can't you see how this works? My brother made sure he told me to be nobody's fool before he died. And that's why Sonia had to be the fall guy. She didn't know I already knew about her and my brother. I've been working for Jerol, too."

Too-reel looked at Deceive and smiled.

"What's so goddamn funny?"

"You are. I already knew about you. You did a great job at the interrogation, but I was already on to you. You fucked up when you shorted the drop-off money. That's what confirmed my suspicions. You knew they were going to raid it so it wouldn't have mattered if it was short because no one was supposed to know. But you didn't know one thing. I always double check the money before I send it out, and you were the only one I had said something to about moving it up two days earlier. Then when I heard you knew about Vanessa being an agent, I knew it had to be you. As far as your brother goes, I knew about him, too. His name was on Jeff's case, too. It wasn't a robbery that killed him, just made to look like one so the DA wouldn't put any more pressure on my peoples. That nigga had to go."

"So you were behind my brother's death?" Deceive asked with a dumbfounded look on her face.

"He was behind his own death."

"I'm going to kill you!"

Deceive advanced on Too-reel with her gun aimed at his head.

POW! POW! POW! POW!

"Get away from my man, bitch!" Vanessa turned the corner, holding a smoking gun in her hand. The shots spun Deceive around and knocked her to the floor. She couldn't believe she was shot as she touched her side and looked at her fingers covered in her own blood. When she looked up and saw Vanessa with the gun, she looked across to Jerol. Deceive coughed, and blood splashed from her nose and mouth.

"You're not supposed to be here." Deceive barely got the words out. Jerol froze in his chair from all the bloodshed.

"How do you think Too-reel knew about this place?" Vanessa asked. "I knew there was something funny going on after I looked at your record and it didn't seem right. It said you got arrested on drug and murder charges and nothing else happened. You were never prosecuted, and I thought that was a little funny. I never did like your pretty ass anyway. And you can keep your badge, Jerol. I quit, you tight-ass son of a bitch!"

Vanessa helped Too-reel to his feet and was turning to leave when two shots flew over her head. She pushed Too-reel outside the room as she dove in mid-air and fired three more shots at Deceive. One of the bullets struck Deceive in the head, killing her instantly.

As Vanessa was getting up from the floor, Jerol stood up from his chair. He stared at Vanessa as he stuck his hand inside his smoker's jacket. She pointed her gun at him, but when he removed his hand and looked at it, it was already covered in blood. He fell over face first onto the desk.

Vanessa hurried Too-reel out of the room and helped him down the stairs and out of the house. She knew it wouldn't be long before the place was crawling with cops.

Chapter 21

"Ice, get everyone together and meet me at the spot, now!" Too-reel told him over the phone.

"Yo, you a'ight? You sound a little fucked up."

"I'm good. Just do what I asked. Get Tashiba and Man, too. They need to hear this."

"You want me to hit Deceive, too?"

"She's not going to be there." Too-reel ended the call as Ice looked at his phone, trying to make sense out of what he had just heard.

"Who was that?"

"Too-reel. He wants everyone to meet him at the spot."

"That don't sound too good."

"I know. He said Deceive wasn't going to be there."

"I guess we won't have time for a quickie."

"Nah," Ice replied as he looked over at Man, lying naked in his bed.

After making a few more calls, Ice had everyone at the spot. As he, Man, Tashiba, Hype, and Blue walked in, they saw trails of blood leading to the other room. Ice and Man both pulled out their guns. Ice approached the door and leaned his head on it to see what he could hear from the other room.

"Ahhh!" he heard someone yell as he turned the doorknob and kicked the door in with his gun leading the way, SWAT-style. When he entered the room, he saw Too-reel seated in a chair with Vanessa holding something bloody in her hands.

"What the fuck's going on?" Ice pointed his gun at Vanessa. She didn't pay him any attention as she continued to try to stop Too-reel's wound from bleeding by applying pressure to it.

"I'm good, Ice. Put down the gun."

Everyone else rushed into the room to see what was going on. Vanessa's clothes were covered in blood as she tended to her child's father.

"I want everyone to take a seat. I have something to tell y'all."

"Shit, I'm standing for this," Man replied as everyone else stood still. They knew one way or the other, they were about to receive some bad news.

"So be it. What I'm about to tell y'all is some real deep shit, so no one ask any questions until I'm finished."

Too-reel closed his eyes and tried to block out the pain from his wound, but also the pain he was about to cause to those who loved him and cherished him the most.

"Deceive is dead, Vanessa is an undercover agent, and I've been working with the Feds for the past few months."

As plainly as he had said it, it was like he was speaking a different language because they didn't understand him.

"Did you just say Deceive is dead?" Tashiba asked.

"And Vanessa is the Feds?" Hype added.

"And what?" Ice screamed.

"Everything I just said is the truth. Deceive was the leak. She—"

"I don't believe that!" Man cut Too-reel off.

"Listen, she had us all fooled. Her brother was on my man Jeff's case, and Sonia and him were working for the DA over five years ago. When Bankroll died, Sonia disappeared on them, but they tracked her down and cornered her. She didn't want Deceive to find out about her brother like that, but Deceive already knew about it and used it against Sonia to make her look like the leak."

"That's bullshit!" Man shouted.

"It's true," Tashiba replied with tears in her eyes. "I heard Sonia tell Deceive that before she shot her that night. And the other day, I overheard her talking to someone named Jerol about how Vanessa was a cop. I thought she was just being paranoid because of the thing with Sonia, but it all makes sense now."

"Why didn't you say anything to me?" Man asked.

"I thought she was just tripping." The tears flowed freely down Tashiba's face. Man was in shock from all this new information. She just stood there, looking at Tashiba.

"What about this bitch and you?" Ice spat.

"Vanessa has been helping me piece this thing together while I tried to find a way out of my situation. They picked me up two months ago and had my moms cuffed and was going to charge her with money laundering. Now, everyone here knows I'll kill and die for this shit, but I couldn't let my moms suffer behind my hands. So, I agreed to cooperate to buy some time. In the process of trying to find a way out, I found out a lot of other things. My eyes were opened to the way they've been really playing the game. These streets aren't the same anymore. They're not the streets we grew up hearing about. The codes have been broken, the players have changed, and there is no more honor in it. Everyone is doing them. The riders are the few and the proud and they, too, are dying slowly. They used me as bait to say, 'Hey, if we can get him to snitch, then it will be a'ight for you to snitch.'

"One thing I know is that they didn't realize they would teach me something in the process. What we have here is rare and very special. You are the last of a dying breed. Never forget where you've come from. They're so many snakes in the grass, I've almost lost my trust and faith that there are still real niggas out there who will stand and hold their own. There is a war going on out there, and no one is safe from it. We are all ready to do time if we have to, but what about when you're doing time and everyone has forgotten about you and life goes on? When everything you've worked for crumbles, when the ones you love betray you?"

"You mean like you have?" Blue whispered with rage in his eyes. It was at that moment, Too-reel understood how Jeff felt when he'd tried telling Too-reel the truth.

"I haven't betrayed y'all. That is why I'm here, telling you this. I'm here to face my punishment. I'm no different from anyone else that breaks the rules. I did it to save my mother, which is no excuse, or in many cases, just an excuse. Ice, nothing has changed. Blue, it's your turn to lead them into the future. I want y'all to learn from what happened to me so y'all will be ready and protect the ones you love. We are not immune to this deadly virus. The love we have for each other, in the end, will be our weakness. That's what Sonia and me were afraid of. I can't tell you not to love, just don't get blinded by it. This is not the end, just a beginning. They will come after you, and the people you least expect will turn on you. Be prepared. We will ride and die with honor."

Too-reel stood and walked to the middle of the room. He faced his shattered team with a smile and his arms spread to the side of him. He gave Blue and Ice each a gun he was holding in each hand as he backed away from them. "The only thing I ask of y'all is to let my child know what kind of father he had."

He looked over at Vanessa. "Tell them I didn't abandon them."

"No! What are you doing?" Vanessa ran in front of Too-reel, blocking his body with hers. "No, I'm not going to let you do this. I'm not raising no child on my own, no!" Vanessa turned around and gripped Too-reel, hugging him tightly.

"Please, Vanessa. This is the only way I know. I'd rather die with honor than live with shame."

"No! No! No! What about us? Don't do this!"

"It's the only way I know, baby. Please." Tears began to streak down Too-reel's face as he held Vanessa. When he looked up at his crew, they were all teary eyed. He motioned for Man and Tashiba to come get Vanessa. As they walked over to Vanessa, she surprisingly let go of him and hugged the two girls as she sobbed uncontrollably.

"Ice, Blue, y'all know what to do." Ice gripped his gun and began to slowly raise it toward Too-reel, holding his head down. Blue pointed the nine he had received from Too-reel and cocked it back. A tear ran down his face as he raised it toward his mentor.

As Blue and Ice stood there with their guns both pointed at Too-reel, time seemed to stop for a brief moment. Too-reel remembered his life and the final lessons he had learned. *So this is what it comes down to*, he thought. *It's almost like I was playing a losing hand from the beginning.* He glanced back at Vanessa one last time before he heard two shots ring out.

"Jerol! Jerol!" Brody yelled as he rolled Jerol over and checked for a pulse. He found a weak one as he flipped out his phone and dialed 911.

"Nooo!" Jerol barely got out the word as he tried to move his hand up, only to have it fall back to the floor.

"What?" Brody placed an ear close to Jerol's mouth as he spoke again.

"Hang up," he whispered.

"What?" Brody replied as the 911 operator came on the line.

"Nine-one-one, how may I help you?" Jerol shook his head from side to side as he looked into Brody's eyes. Brody clicked off the call.

"What do you want me to do?" Jerol opened his hand and a

bloody card fell from it. Brody picked it up and looked at it. There was only one number on it. It had a Mexico exchange. Brody dialed the number and waited as it rang.

"Hola," a man's voice answered.

"Jerol Highmon gave me this number. He has been injured and needs help."

"Where are you, my friend?"

"In the house in New York."

"Someone will be there soon."

"Señor Dei'z, your car is ready," a voice said in the background before the line went dead.

-The End-

COMING SOON

BOSS
COVER REVEAL SOON!

Order Information
Wynn Publishing
P.O. Box 40411
Raleigh, N.C. 27629
www.wynnpubication.com
wynnpublications@yahoo.com
Contact: 984-220-2638

We accept Visa, MasterCard,
Ammex and PayPal

SEND MONEY ORDER/CHECK TO:	WYNN PUBLICATIONS P.O. Box 40411 2777 Brentwood RD. Raleigh, NC 27604		

NAME			
ADDRESS			
CITY			
STATE	ZIP		
EMAIL			

BOOK TITLE	PRICE EACH	QUANTITY	TOTAL
BEHIND THE MASK	12.00		
FALSE	12.00		
MY BROTHERS KEEPER PT 1	12.00		
MY BROTHERS KEEPER PT 2	12.00		
A WHORE'S CONSCIENCE	12.00		
TAINTED	12.00		

THANK YOU FOR YOUR BUSINESS	TOTAL	
	SHIPPING & HANDLING	6.00
	FINAL TOTAL	

www.ingramcontent.com/pod-product-compliance
Lightning Source LLC
Chambersburg PA
CBHW071350170626
46811CB00003B/1071